chasing MIA

lauren michelle

chasing MIA

Facebook: Author Lauren Michelle
Instagram: Lauren Michelle Pratt

Editor: Lisa Cerasoli
Interior Design: Lisa Cerasoli & Danielle Canfield
Cover: Sarah Hansen, www.okaycreations.com

—Sophomore book is a winner—
"Lauren Michelle, I am giving you a standing ovation. You nailed it with this book. I loved everything about this book. The characters, the storyline, everything just flowed. Great job. I look forward to your next one."

—Jane

—Unable to put this one down!—
"I read this in a day because I couldn't bear to put it down. The story moves right along and it moves you with it, making you laugh, ache, love, hurt, and I'll only admit this here...cry. It had me from the beginning and I couldn't come up for air until I finished the last line. It has everything I think a book needs to be successful, and I can't give you a single reason not to read it."

—Carol Blodgett

—Raven and Eric—
"He's got issues. Serious ones. Ones keeping him from fully opening himself up to anyone. Even his BFF Raven. This is a heart-wrenching story about healing. Well written and entertaining to read."

—Rebelle

chasing MIA

ONE

a m e l i a

There's something very scary yet refreshingly liberating about not knowing who the hell you are or where you're heading in life. As I make my way from my hometown of Lindsborg, Kansas, to Austin, Texas, I'm currently experiencing this phenomenon. Pushing my Aviators up over my eyes, I'm closing in on the last leg of the trip. With my windows down and my dark brown hair whipping around my face, nothing but the tastes and smells of my new city infuse my senses.

Freedom.

It's October, which is my favorite time of year to make this drive. The vibrant colors of autumn in the Midwest are nothing short of spectacular—rich shades of orange, red, and yellow. Once in a while, Mother Nature will treat you to some purples and pinks. Lucky for me, this is one of those years.

Just as I'm merging onto South Mopac, my phone lights up with Raven's smiling face. Raven is my very loyal, and very impatient, best friend. I grab the phone and slide my finger across the screen.

"Yes?"

"When are you going to get here already?"

I roll my eyes but secretly smile. She called me fifteen minutes ago asking the same thing. I wasn't joking when I said she was impatient. This woman has high standards for everything, and for her, bigger means better. Probably a good thing she lives in Texas.

"I just hopped on Mopac, so I'll be there in less than twenty minutes."

"My God, that long? All this waiting is killing me."

"I know. It's so much harder for you than it is for me—the one making the actual drive," I say sarcastically.

"Yes, it is. So glad we understand each other on that. Oh, and before I forget, Eric called. New game plan: we're going to unpack and head straight to his place. He's having a few friends over and he offered to cook. I'm thinking this needs to become the norm, you know, him cooking for us all the time."

"Agreed. I'm starving. Maybe we can go there, eat first, and unpack later?"

"Sure, works for me."

"Awesome. I'll see you soon."

"Okay, bye."

I hang up the phone and crank up the music, letting The Black Keys carry me through the rest of my journey.

Five songs later, I'm pulling into Raven's apartment complex. I punch in the code she gave me via text, the gate slowly opens, and I cruise on through. Lifting my sunglasses onto my head, I keep my eyes peeled for her building number. Spotting it, I park in the closest space, turn off the car, and pop the trunk. I shoot her a text letting her know I'm here, asking her to help me haul boxes. No more than thirty seconds later, the sound of heels striking against the pavement creeps ever closer. Then comes the screech I know so well....

"Ahhhh, Mia!"

I turn around and am nearly trampled. Laughing at her uncontained excitement, I hug Raven hard before releasing. Ravenna Bellotti was raised in a big, Italian-Catholic family, and like any true Italian, style and good food are no joking matters to her. She can cook with the best of them and has brains and personality to rival her beauty. Her parents own Bellotti's—a fine Italian restaurant here in Austin that's run primarily by family. She's currently studying business management and is set to graduate from St. Edward's in May.

"I've missed you so much."

"Don't even get me started. I've been waiting for you to get here all day. Here, let me help you with those boxes, then we'll head to Eric's. I'll drive."

I walk into the apartment to find everything sleek, clean, and orderly. *Seriously, who the hell lives like this?* There's a spacious dining room complete with a table and chairs. In the center of the table, an array of dark, colorful candles are lined up neatly. The living room has high, vaulted ceilings with an open kitchen attached. The walls are painted a warm taupe, the carpeting is light and creamy and looks brand new. The dark brown couches are decorated with rustic orange and red pillows on either side, and a gorgeous, mahogany coffee table sits in the middle. It's huge, Texas huge. A large flat screen TV is mounted on the opposite wall. Beneath it, there are shelves filled with movies and books—all in alphabetical order.

The kitchen has granite counter tops—*at least I think they're granite*—stainless steel appliances, dark cupboards, and a center island lined with bar stools on one side. The laundry room, full bathroom, and then our two bedrooms are all down the hallway. We have a room for laundry. I'm well aware that most college students do not live like this. Hell, the house I grew up in isn't even half as nice as my new "humble" abode.

Looking around, I spy many framed photos on the walls. I come across one that was taken a few years back of Raven, Eric, and me at one of her birthday parties. Eric is positioned in the middle, as usual. He has his arms around us, and we are all giving the camera our most ridiculous faces. It's one of those photos where we were trying to portray how totally cool and laidback we thought we were, but really we come off like idiots. I wish I could tell you that we've grown into well-rounded, respectable adults.

Eric, Raven, and I go way back to the days of braces, awkward first kisses, and training bras. Yes, Eric was there for my first bra. He wasn't happy about it, but the three of us spent every single day together that first summer...and so he was there. I was too mortified to ask my dad to go bra shopping with me, so Raven stepped up to the plate, and tackled the challenge like a pro. Even then, she was determined to find me the best training bra that my money could buy.

Now that my dad's gone, the two of them are the only real connections I have here. When you grow up and leave home, you realize that you *can* choose your family despite being told otherwise. Raven and Eric are my family. The three of us hit it off so well, and meld together so perfectly, that I often wonder why I couldn't have met these two crazy souls sooner—like at birth.

After my parents divorced when I was a kid, my dad moved to Austin. I made sure to visit him every chance I had. That was how I met Raven and Eric. I loved spending time with him, and I would've given anything to live here, but he didn't want to uproot my life and all I knew back home. Plus, he didn't want to take me away from my mom. So, I stayed behind and watched her spiral into a life of guilt, regret, and alcoholism. To say that I was the parent in that house would be the understatement of the century. I was trapped working two jobs and put off continuing college in order to keep the bills paid. In my dad's defense, he had no idea how bad things became after he left.

There came a point when I realized that I had to start living my life for myself, and not for other people, even Mom. For me, there had been one too many sacrifices, one too many fights, and one too many times of not feeling safe in my own home that brought me to that conclusion. I quit both jobs, packed my things, and finally did what I should've done years ago—drove to my "family" without a second thought. Now, at twenty-two, I feel like I can start living my life again. Twenty-two is incredibly young in the grand scheme of things, but most days, I feel forty.

"Raven, your place is gorgeous." I exhale the words.

"*Our* place," she corrects, "and thank you."

She grabs one of my boxes and leads me down the hallway. "Your room is the one on the right. I'm sorry there isn't more furniture, but I didn't know what all you would be bringing or shipping. We can always go furniture shopping this weekend if you need more stuff."

My bedroom has a full bed with a nightstand next to it and a big open closet for my clothes. "That isn't necessary, Raven. This is more than enough, really. I don't know how to thank you for letting me move in with you on such short notice."

"Hey, don't mention it. That's what friends are for. Now let's get the rest of your boxes up here and get ready to head out."

After we clear everything out of the car, I make one last trip down to grab a spare outfit out of the back seat that I keep for desperate times. I never knew when I was going to come home from work only to end up arguing with my mother and getting kicked out of the house for a night—the house that I was paying the bills for. The irony is not lost. I grab my black tube top, skinny jeans, spare underwear, and red Chucks—perfect for the first night in my new life.

I take the fastest shower known to man, washing off all of the disgusting travel grime. After I'm fully dressed, I dry and straighten my hair and then apply some makeup to my overly, tired face. I load up my hazel eyes with some eyeliner and mascara, giving them a sharp intensity. If you haven't already guessed, I'm not one for skirts, heels, anything pink, and I rarely dress to impress. It's not my style. I'll go for jeans and sneakers any day of the week. I lace up my shoes and grab my phone and wallet. That way we can stop at the store and buy some beer on the way—my treat.

Eric only lives about five minutes away, so we arrive in no time.

"Y'all are late!" a male voice shouts. I look up to find Eric watching us from the balcony.

"First of all, it's *you guys* are late. Secondly, we most certainly are not late, you twat!" I shout back.

He shakes his head and laughs. "Man, I missed you, Strawberry."

The dude has called me Strawberry for years. Coming from any other guy, that term of endearment would be hella creepy, but because it's Eric and I love him to pieces, I allow it.

"Come on, let's go." Raven chuckles.

I open the door and step into a sea of people. Smells of sweat and alcohol permeate the apartment. The kitchen counter is littered with tequila bottles and mixers. I walk over to the fridge, weaving my way through the masses, and set the beer inside. Robin Thicke's "Take It Easy On Me" is seeping through the speakers, and groups of people are dancing seductively in the living room. I immediately feel uncomfortable, unhook my Aviators from my tube top, and slide them over my eyes—the perfect hiding place.

Yeah, I'm *that* girl—the one who uses sunglasses to diffuse awkwardness. I don't handle intense emotional situations well, so my sunglasses protect me from those—at least, that's what I keep telling myself.

I close the refrigerator door and turn to make my way out onto the balcony. Suddenly, a bleach blonde in sky-high heels comes crashing into me from around the corner, effectively spilling part of her drink down my top. *You've got to be kidding.* I tense up and clamp my mouth shut to keep from yelling. Thankfully, my shirt is black and not white.

Blondie staggers back, tipsy, and grabs ahold of the kitchen table to steady herself. "Oops, my bad," she sarcastically snipes.

I narrow my eyes and adjust my top. Just as I'm about to step forward and say something, I feel a small hand wrap around my arm. Raven comes up and positions herself beside me.

"Hey, are you all right?" she asks.

"Fine," I respond through clenched teeth. Raven turns her head to glance Drunk Chick and then back at me. Doesn't take her long to sense the tidal waves of tension rolling off my body.

"Let's go say hi to Eric," she suggests, pulling me away.

We move past the blonde, who's now on a mission to refill her drink. *Yeah, because you really need another one of those, sweetheart.*

Raven opens the sliding door and we step out onto the balcony. The breeze feels so good against my skin. The scent of smoke fills the air, like a pile of burning leaves. Eric turns to look at us, and his face lights up with a mischievous grin. He sets the tongs down, strides over, and swoops me up into a hug that causes any anger I have left to evaporate. I smile and wrap my arms around his neck, squeezing him back.

"Missed you," he whispers in my ear, lifting me off the ground.

"Missed you more," I respond.

He sets me down, removes my sunglasses, and slides them on top of his head. He totally did that on purpose; he knows about my little quirk. He then pulls Raven into a warm embrace.

"Eric, what are you doing grilling out on the balcony? It's against the fire code to do that out here," I remind him.

"Nonsense. Just like whoring around, if nobody knows about it, or says anything about it, then it didn't happen."

He has a point.

Eric Hansen is a shameless womanizer who comes from an even more dysfunctional background than me. We're uniquely bonded to each other—not just because of our ties with Raven, but because damage understands damage. It's like a magnet to a fridge. People like us tend to gravitate toward one another without being consciously aware of it.

As for his personal attributes, I find that he's cute, charming, and easygoing. The fact that he knows these things about himself makes him lethal. He has a heart of gold, the silver tongue of a serpent, and the face of an angel. His blond hair and crystal-blue eyes only add to the complexity and allure that is Eric. He loves women, and women love him. Yes, he goes through them like underwear, changing his tastes daily, but he's honest about what he does. And when the next morning rolls around, the woman-in-question doesn't find cab fare taped to her forehead like some attraction he paid to ride at a carnival. Instead, she's greeted with a latté, fresh from Starbucks.

"What if someone calls and complains?" Raven asks.

"Then we better pray the cops like my kabobs, otherwise we're screwed."

He turns back around to pull the lid up on the grill. A display of hot dogs, brats, and kabobs meet my eyes, and my mouth waters at the sight.

"Anything I can help with?" I ask.

"Naw, I got it covered. Y'all just grab a drink and enjoy yourselves."

I turn to ask Raven what she would like to drink when, through my periphery, I see the sliding door to the balcony open up. Just as I turn my head, I'm met with a stunning pair of sapphire eyes that halt any and all breathing. *Wow.*

His eyes are sharp, intense, hypnotic. I notice he has a scar above his left eyebrow. His thick dark hair is long, but not too long, slightly curling out beneath his ears. He's wearing jeans and a white, V-neck tee that showcases some dark curls on his chest. Crawling up his right forearm are some intricate tattoos.

I watch his eyes travel from my hips to my face as he slowly takes in my appearance. A shy smile appears, causing two dimples to form on his cheeks. He has this amazing five o'clock shadow thing going on, making him look a little more rugged. I instantly entertain the thought of how glorious his face would feel like between my legs.

Jesus, Mia. Snap out of it!

Sliding past Raven and me, Mr. Tall, Dark, and Sinful hands Eric an empty plate that I didn't even realize he'd been holding. I inconspicuously let out a breath and avert my attention back to Raven, who's trying to suppress her smile. She's giving me *that look*—

letting me know through the powers of best friend telepathy that I'm busted.

"Thanks, man," Eric says, grabbing the plate from him.

"No problem." He shifts his gaze. "Hey, Raven," he greets casually.

"Hey, yourself," she retorts.

His eyes find mine again, and that smile reappears. "I don't think we've met, I'm Chase." He offers his hand.

I calmly reach for it, even though inside I'm freaking out. I give him a nice, firm handshake and notice that his hands are dry and rough.

"Amelia Foster, but everyone calls me Mia," I reply.

"Nice to meet you, Mia."

"Likewise." I step back and bury my hands in my pockets in an attempt to calm my nerves.

Chase is about a head or so taller than me. He's cut and toned in all the right areas, but not overly muscular. He's all man with the exception of those dimples that give him a younger look. To some, he probably seems dangerous, but I'm not getting those kinds of vibes. Perhaps I just don't want to see what's right in front of me because I'm so intrigued. That wouldn't be an unfair assessment at this point.

"So, how do you two know each other?" He motions between Eric and me.

"She's my lover," Eric deadpans.

I roll my eyes. "Don't believe a word he says. I cut him off at the pass years ago. We've been friends for a long time, though. I met him through Raven when I was visiting my dad here one summer."

"Yeah. You wanna see the only two women to ever friend zone me? You're looking at 'em," Eric points to us with the tongs. "Just imagine what that did to my ego. I was completely and utterly heartbroken when I couldn't have them. And I don't just mean together." He clasps a hand over his heart playfully.

"I can only imagine," Chase says, his tone completely serious.

Okay, now I feel uneasy. *Too personal...need sunglasses. Dammit, Eric!*

"Please, Eric, putting you in the friend zone was the best decision that we could've made for this friendship to last," Raven points out, ignoring the sudden shift in the air.

"Yeah, because everyone wins in that scenario," he says dryly.

"You said that you met Eric while you were visiting your dad for the summer...do you not live here?" Chase asks, smoothly bringing the conversation back to us.

"I'm originally from Kansas, but I've recently moved down here—today, actually."

He raises both of his eyebrows. "Really? Did you move here to be closer to your dad?"

My chest tightens at the thought of my dad, and I contemplate how to explain my current circumstances. "Not exactly. I'm looking to start over. Meet new people, try new things, finish college, and find a job. Raven graciously offered to let me stay with her for a while until I get my situation figured out."

"Thank you for that, Raven," he looks at her approvingly, as if he were her boss and she just landed a big client.

Just then, my favorite drunk blonde comes barreling through the door and into Chase—effectively ruining our staring contest. She seems to have a really bad habit of running into people. "Hey, baby, there you are," she purrs. "I brought you a beer. Figured you were getting thirsty and needed something to drink."

Gross. Feminists everywhere are outraged. If I were wearing a bra under this shirt, it'd be burning.

Now, this is a tricky position. Part of me feels slightly jealous, but the rational side of me understands that I have no right to be. I've known this guy for two whole minutes. It's certainly not a knife to the heart or a swift kick to the gut, but I'm not going to lie, it's a letdown. So I do what almost any other girl would do in this situation, I put my guard up and immediately write him off.

Grabbing my sunglasses off Eric's head and excusing myself, I make my way back into the apartment. With Raven right on my heels, I head for the kitchen to grab a spare plate for food and try to enjoy the rest of my evening.

TWO

c h a s e

It's been a long day. Between work kicking my ass and my sister blowing up my phone, I've barely had any down time. It's one of the reasons why I've been looking forward to Eric's party tonight. By the time I arrive, there's already a ton of people here. Most of them I know, or at least recognize from other run-ins. Striding into the kitchen, the first thing I go for is an ice-cold beer. The second thing I go for—*Christa.*

Christa and I have a very casual and convenient relationship. I've known her for a couple of years now, and she's always down for a good time. She's looking sexy as hell tonight in that dress. My mind instantly wanders to how lovely those long legs of hers will look when they're wrapped around my torso.

Downing my beer, I dispose of the bottle and walk over. I fist a handful of her hair and lean down to press a kiss to her lips.

"Hey, you," she says, smiling up at me. "I thought you weren't coming until later."

"I got off work a little early," I explain.

It was a slow night at the bar for a change. My boss let me go early, knowing I'd worked at my other job this morning. I'm like a superhero living a double life. By day, I'm a respectable carpenter who creates, repairs, and refinishes furniture for my dad's company. By night, I'm a part-time bartender who spends his time slinging drinks and philandering around, getting into all sorts of fun trouble. I work hard, and I play harder. I don't have to work two jobs, but the truth is I actually enjoy it. I love the extra money coming in, and I like leading a very busy life.

Just as I'm about to lean in for another kiss, Eric opens the sliding door and scans the apartment until he spots me.

"Chase, can you grab me a clean plate for the food?" he yells over the music.

I nod and turn my attention to Christa. "Be right back."

I release my hold on her hair and head to the kitchen in search of a plate. Not seeing any on the counter, I start snooping through cupboards.

The door to the apartment swings open and I turn around to see Raven strolling in with a friend I don't recognize. Raven is one of my good, female friends. I know what you're probably thinking, and no—I've never slept with her. There are two main reasons for that. First and foremost, Eric has feelings for her. Secondly, she's too high maintenance for my tastes.

The two of us met through Eric years ago. He and I went to the same high school. Even back then, eighteen-year-old Eric had the hots for fourteen-year-old Raven. Go ahead and let that one sink in. Four years is no big deal now, but back then, it was nothing short of a charming, twisted perversion—as are the best experiences in life...and the worst.

I watch as her mystery friend breezes past me and opens the fridge. I can't catch a solid glimpse of her face yet because she's turned away, but she has this tomboy-meets-hipster thing happening. She's in a pair of tight jeans that really complement her ass, but it's not over-the-top. It's anything but over-the-top, making her even more attractive.

When Christa comes around the corner and spills her drink on my soon-to-be new friend, I cringe. I hate it when other people I'm associated with make themselves look stupid.

"Oops, my bad," Christa taunts.

The girl tightens up like she's ready for a fight. I move to step in between them, but Raven beats me to it. Good, I'm not in the mood for drama tonight. The girls step out onto the balcony together and Christa stops at the counter to refill her cup.

"What the hell was that about?"

"Nothing. She was in my way, that's all."

Seriously? I grab a plate and head for the balcony to apologize to that girl.

When I step outside, our eyes briefly lock, and I instantly regret following her out here because I know how utterly screwed I am. But since I'm already here, I hand Eric the plate and properly introduce myself.

I come to find that her name is Amelia, and she just moved to Austin. Currently, she's crashing with Raven. This is good. This I can work with. She's close friends with Raven and Eric, which means she'll also be hanging around me from time to time.

Just when the conversation starts to get good, Christa comes running into me and I mentally curse her for the timing. I have no doubt she's done this on purpose to send a false message to Mia. It's the first time where her presence is not only unwelcome, it's irritating. I look at Mia and notice the brief flash in her eyes and then her entire demeanor changes. Her stance becomes rigid, and her facial expression screams "fuck off!" She looks uncomfortable. I don't blame her. But before I can apologize, she's sliding past me to get through the door. Raven follows her inside.

"What just happened?" Eric asks.

"I don't know, man," I lie. One second everything was going smoothly, the next it all went straight to hell. I don't need Eric, or anyone else, trying to get involved. They'll only end up making things worse. If I'm not careful, I'll blow my chance with Mia before I even get one.

Eric fills up the plate and goes inside, giving Christa and me some much-needed privacy. I grab the beer from her hand and try to figure out how to get rid of her without sounding like an ass. Most guys would never pass up a night of guaranteed sex, and honestly, I usually wouldn't either. But this is an exception. Mia was interested. I saw it in her eyes.

I'd also be lying if I said her whole stand-off attitude didn't make me want her more. I already found her intriguing to begin with, and now that she's trying to make herself unattainable, well, there's nothing more attractive than that. *Challenge accepted.*

Christa boldly presses her body into mine and cups my face in her hands. She looks into my eyes, smiling a little too eagerly, feeling the effects of the alcohol. "Wanna get out of here soon? I know you just got here, but I'm ready to go whenever you are." She trails a finger down my chest.

"Did you drive here yourself, or did you come with a friend?"

"I drove. Why?" She looks puzzled.

Shit. I can't make her drive herself home like this. "Grab your purse along with whatever else you brought and meet me by the front door in two minutes. I'm taking you home."

"You're staying the night, right?"

"Not tonight. I'm tired and you're tipsy."

"Those things have never stopped you before," she says sharply.

I let out a frustrated sigh and run my hands through my hair. I'm trying to stay patient, but I don't do well with neediness and whining. I also don't like explaining my actions to someone else. It's the exact reason I've chosen to stay single for so long.

"Babe, just grab your stuff and meet me by the door. We can talk about this in the car. I don't want to argue with you out here."

"Forget it. I'll drive myself home."

She tries to move past me. I reach out, grasp her arm, and pull her back.

"Why are you acting like this?"

"Acting like what? You're the one who doesn't see a good thing standing right in front of you. Instead of coming home with me, you'd rather stay here and try to bullshit your way into that girl's pants. Am I right?"

I glare and she rips her arm from my grasp.

"Yeah, I saw the way you two were looking at each other. Chase, you don't even know her. All of a sudden, she shows up out of nowhere and you're going to treat me like shit? How noble of you," she snaps.

Okay, now she's starting to piss me off. I take a deep breath and step toward her. "Don't you dare sit there and try to turn this around. You knew from the get-go that I wasn't looking for anything serious, and you wholeheartedly agreed. This has been working well for us, and until now, there's never been a problem with overstepping a boundary."

"Excuse me? I'm not overstepping a boundary."

"Yes, you are. You're trying to hold me accountable for my actions, as if you are my girlfriend or my mother, and you're neither. You are a friend, Christa. Don't get me wrong, we've had a lot of fun together, but I don't answer to you."

By this point, she's fuming. I can almost see the smoke billowing out of her ears—I don't give a shit. She's not going to make me feel guilty about this. I take another sip of beer and put some space between us. She just stands there, staring, like she doesn't understand how I could turn her down for the night.

"Maybe it's best if someone else drives me home," she suggests. "We both need to sleep on this. I'm sure we'll feel better in the morning."

No, what I need is to get her out of here and talk to Mia some more. That, and another beer would help. "Do you have someone who can take you home? If not, you know I will."

She relaxes a little. "I know, but I think I'm going to call my sister and ask her to pick me up instead."

I nod. "Okay. If you need the ride, let me know."

"Call me tomorrow?"

"Will do."

She opens the door and heads inside. I decide to stay out here for a couple more minutes to cool down.

Finishing off my second beer, I lean across the railing and listen to the familiar sounds of Austin—the breeze sifting through the air, the occasional sound of cars passing by, the voices being carried up to the balcony. What I love about Austin is that it's city-like enough to be busy and thriving, but you don't have to drive very far before you're breathing clean, country air. Out there, it's peaceful and secluded—best of both worlds.

A couple minutes pass by and I'm feeling significantly more relaxed. I walk back inside and look around, spotting Mia. She's sitting next to Raven on the couch. I stroll up, sit on the other side of Raven, and place my arm on the back of the couch. Raven turns her head, and I give her a pleading look, one that tells her that I'd really like some alone time with her friend.

Taking the hint, she clears her throat and starts to make her way off the couch, but not before Mia's hand comes crashing down on her knee. "Don't even think about it, Rave," she warns.

Raven stays hunched over, looking back and forth between us. I take the opportunity to crane my neck and watch Mia. She's deliberately avoiding eye contact.

"Well, this should be fun," Raven says, sitting back. I really wanted to do this without an audience, but seeing as how Mia isn't letting that happen, I modify my expectations.

"So, Mia, what day are you available to go out with me this week? I was thinking dinner and maybe something fun afterward?"

She leans forward. "Don't flatter yourself."

"You're cute when you're mad, you know that?" I've only just met her, but I already feel comfortable enough to push her buttons. I know I'm coming on strong, but soon she'll see it as part of my charm.

She scowls and slides her Aviators over her eyes, unimpressed.

When it's apparent she's going to continue to ignore my advances, I try a different approach. "Raven, could you do me a favor and tell your friend here that I'd like to apologize for what happened between us earlier on the balcony? I'd also like to apologize on Christa's behalf for her attitude in the kitchen. That was uncalled for."

Mia leans forward again; the scowl is gone. "You know, Chase, I'm a big girl. I can take care of myself, and luckily, I don't need my friends to be my messengers. I appreciate your apology, but there's nothing you need to be apologizing for, I assure you. And as for...Christa...is it? If she wants to apologize to me, then she can do it herself instead of sending her boyfriend to clean up her mess."

"First of all, I'm not her boyfriend. Second of all, yes, I do owe you an apology. What happened on the balcony was misleading in more ways than one—so I'm sorry for that. I'm not a total asshole, despite what you may think."

She looks up at me, confused. "Chase, I barely know you. You don't owe me anything. And I wasn't being misled. It's pretty clear what's going on between you two. I just don't want to get in the middle of it, that's all."

Okay, I know I just said that I hate explaining myself, but.... I like her. If that means I have to bend a little, so be it.

"See, that's the thing—yes there *was* something casual going on between Christa and I—but that wasn't what was misleading. Where I went wrong was when I let you walk off, making you think that I wasn't interested in you."

I let out a frustrated sigh as I try to find the right words. "We...I...you know what, screw it. Let me take you out to dinner Monday night, and I'll tell you all about it. Sound good?"

She lets out a hard laugh. "That won't be necessary but thank you."

"Come on, you know you want to. Admit it, you were just as intrigued out there as I was, before Christa came out and ruined everything."

She gives me a dubious look.

"Don't give me that look. I know I'm right. Just picture it, a nice restaurant with delicious food, even better conversation, drinks...."

"Bellotti's," Raven coughs.

"And let me guess, then we go back to your place afterward?" Mia asks, with a hint of boredom.

"As amazing as that sounds, I'll be on my best behavior. Promise."

She folds her hands in her lap, like she's mulling it over.

"You know, all of my instincts are telling me that this is a bad idea, but I also believe in giving someone a fair shot to prove me wrong."

"Give me one night to show you that I'm really not that bad of a guy. If the date is horrible, at least you get a free meal out of it. And for the record, I'm persistent. I will keep trying until you give me a couple hours of your time."

She takes a deep breath and looks over at Raven, silently seeking her approval like girls do.

Raven needs to sign-off on this, and if she does, I'll owe her big. She smiles and nods.

Mia's gaze finds mine.

"I need you to give me one good reason why I should. And think twice before you sling bullshit, because I'll see right through it," she says.

Tired of Raven barricading us, I move to sit on the coffee table. I grab Mia's plate, set it down beside me, then seize her sunglasses, slowly pulling them off her face.

She gulps. I fold her sunglasses around the V of my shirt.

Looking into her eyes, I say, "Do you feel that? That's chemistry. You can't tell me there isn't something here. I'd love to stay and argue that I'm worth your time, but only you can decide that. You're going to have to take a chance on me. You said it yourself, remember? You're here to take risks and create a new life. You want to meet new people, try new things. Well, you met me, so are you going to try me?"

She studies me carefully, saying nothing.

"The decision is yours. Just get my number from Eric or Raven and let me know what you decide. Okay?"

She nods ever so slightly.

I stand up and grab her empty plate. Raven is sitting there, staring at me like I'm crazy.

"Raven, always a pleasure."

I make my way to the kitchen. When I'm finished rinsing her plate, I say my goodbyes, grab my keys, and call it a night. I have another long day ahead of me tomorrow, but at least now I have something to look forward to.

THREE

a m e l i a

Chase couldn't take a hint to save his life. I'd given him the cold shoulder, the silent treatment—you name it. He just kept coming back for more. I'm starting to think he's a glutton for punishment, although, his persistence was equally flattering and irritating. When I'd throw a rock, he'd launch a boulder.

Eventually, he ended up with a date. I haven't texted him to confirm it, but we both know I'm going to say yes. How could I not? I found him attractive to begin with, and then he laid into me with that charisma until I caved. It seems that's his secret weapon and he knows it. I'll have to keep that in mind for future reference. Monday is still two days away, so I don't have to text him right away. Even though I've already made up my mind, it couldn't hurt to make him sweat a little.

Suddenly, a knock on my bedroom door interrupts my musings. *Real life always ruins everything.*

"Come in."

Raven opens the door, moseys on in, and plops herself down on my bed, still in pajamas.

"How'd you sleep?"

"Really well. This bed is ridiculously comfy."

"Tell me about it. It's like sleeping on a cloud." She extends her arms and legs out, proceeding to make snow angels on the covers. *What an adorable little weirdo.* She flips onto her stomach and crawls up the bed. When she reaches me, she leans down on her elbow and clasps her head in her palm. Looks like playtime's over.

"Have you heard from your mom yet?"

Annnnd...there it is.

"I don't know. I shut my phone off last night. I'm sure the drunk texts and calls will come pouring in as soon as I turn it on. They always do." It's one of the few consistencies I can count on.

Thankfully, she doesn't press the issue.

"Have you made a decision on whether you're going to give Chase a chance?"

"I have to. The bastard still has my sunglasses."

She laughs. "That was quite a connection y'all formed last night. And quite a speech he gave, if I do say so myself."

"What's the deal with him and Christa? Are they a couple?"

"No. They've never been exclusive. At least, not to my knowledge. He was being honest about that. They have history, though. You should ask Eric because he would know more about their relationship than me. All I know is they've been hooking up for a while now."

Great, I have a potential player on my hands. That's extra drama I don't need. Maybe I should've followed my instincts. Rubbing my eyes, I groan and readjust my body so I'm lying down beside her, my head propped up on a pillow.

"I don't know what to do, Rave. I like him, and I want to go out with him, but there are red flags."

"Mia, you know I would never tell you to go against your gut, but at the same time when you eventually fall for someone, there are always going to be risks and imperfections involved. I think you're so used to being disappointed by your mom that you've put up a wall to protect yourself. Not everyone reverts to their old ways like she does. I'm not saying that Chase's past isn't concerning, but he isn't a bad guy. I could never see him doing anything to hurt you on purpose. Plus, your chemistry is explosive," she says with a giggle.

I know she's right, but deep down I'm skeptical. I can't help it. I've spent a great deal of time building up walls in order to survive my mom. And when I was around Chase last night, he made me feel vulnerable and out of my element. I'm not sure I know how to handle that. Raven is right, though. I have to learn to trust my heart over my gut, and hope that it doesn't come back around to bite me in the ass.

"You know, you really are like the sister I never had."

"I know," she smiles confidently. "Don't worry, if he hurts you, I'll boil his balls."

"Promise?"

"Always." She kisses my forehead and rolls off the bed.

"Where are you going?" I ask, sitting up.

"Gotta get ready for work. I'm on the lunch shift today. Feel free to help yourself to whatever you want. This is your place now, too."

I smile. "Please tell your family hi."

"I will." She steps out of my room and closes the door.

I look around at all of the boxes "decorating" my floor, dreading the unpacking process that lies ahead. With a huff, I pull the covers back and reach over to grab my cell phone off the nightstand. Reluctantly, I turn it on; what's coming my way won't be pretty. Sure enough, my phone begins to vibrate, over and over, from the missed calls and text messages. I see that there are three unread messages from my mom and one from Hadley.

Hadley is my Raven back in Kansas. I owe her a lot. We both went to the same high school, and there were many times when I crashed at her place after my mom kicked me out for the night. Mom was never too fond of me hanging out with her, which only made me like her more. She thought Hadley was a bad influence. That's not entirely false, but some of the best people out there are the ones that push you to take risks. She's actually the one who urged me to move down here. I'm sure that only added another nail to her coffin in my mother's eyes.

I open up the text from Hadley first, not wanting to deal with my mom.

Hadley: *Text me when you get there to let me know you're still alive. Miss you already.*

Me: *Made it down here safely. Will call you later tonight. Got so much to tell you! :)*

My hands begin to tremble. I brace myself as I tap on the three unread messages from my mom.

Mom: *Call me as soon as you get this.*

Mom: *Don't think for one second that you can just walk out on me and ignore my calls. I'm still your mother. Call me!*

Mom: *Mia, this isn't funny. Get your ass home now, otherwise you can find somewhere else to sleep for the night.*

I toss my phone aside, close my eyes, and lean back against the headboard. Feelings of guilt and remorse start to creep up my throat. The ramifications of what I've done start to fully sink in. *I left her behind.* God, what if something bad happens and I'm not there to help? It would be all my fault. Memories from our last fight begin to flash before my mind. I try my best to block it out, but it's pulling me under and there's nothing I can do to stop it.

Nine Days Earlier....

I walk out of her bedroom and down the hallway in the direction of the stairs.

"Don't you dare walk away from me, Amelia Jaymes! Get back here right now!" she yells.

I pick up my pace and rush down the stairs, taking them two at a time. I hear her stomping, coming after me. Once I'm at the bottom of the stairs, I make a swift right and end up in our living room. I turn around, dreading that, at any second, her foot is going to hit that bottom step. My heart is hammering in my chest.

A beat goes by and her bare foot hits the bottom step. She's dressed in the same bathrobe that she's had on for three days. Her hair looks like it hasn't been washed in a week. She has dark hues under her eyes, making her look about ten years older than she actually is. She's holding a bottle of vodka in her left hand and a cigarette in her right. The house reeks of smoke and booze—an unsettling yet familiar scent: home.

"I'm not done talking to you, young lady!" she shouts.

I eye the vodka in her hand warily, knowing all too well that she has a tendency to get aggressive when she's been drinking this much. When you live with an alcoholic, you quickly learn what sets them off and train yourself to prepare for the worst.

"You know, Mia, I'm really sick and tired of you being so ungrateful in my house."

"*Your* house?" I mock.

She glares at me. Her grip tightens around the neck of the bottle. "You best watch your tone with me. This is my house and you live by my rules, understood?"

"Funny, I'm the only one paying the bills to keep us afloat in *your* house," I spit back.

Wafer-thin ice.

Her eyes darken in fury, and she reaches me in three long strides—stopping only two inches from my face. I swallow hard and begin to tremble, afraid of what's coming next. Her towering stance makes me feel like a helpless child again. Her breath reeks. I automatically lean back a couple inches and try to calm my nerves. I have to hold my ground.

"Who the hell are you to speak to me that way? I'm your mother, and you will respect me."

She grabs ahold of my throat and brings me closer. "You know, every time I look at your face, I see him."

This is not a good thing. She hates being reminded of him. All it does is fuel her depression and self-loathing. The more she drinks, the more I look like him. Sounds like a great motivator to quit drinking. *What the hell do I know?*

Acting on impulse, I shove her back.

She drops her cigarette and stumbles, then stares down at the floor impassively for a minute. When it finally clicks that her precious cigarette is wasting away, she makes a dive for it. "You little shit!"

I use this moment of distraction to grab an empty bottle and smash it against the coffee table, holding the broken end in her direction, just in case.

She charges at me but freezes when she sees the bottle in my hand. "Is this your way of threatening me?" she asks in disbelief.

I stand there silently, trying to anticipate her next move.

She spreads her arms wide. "Go ahead. But know this, you take one swing at me, and you're done for."

My eyes widen. This is it—a pivotal moment. I've hit my limit and I can't take anymore. I toss the rest of the bottle on the ground, shattering what's left of it, and feel a rage boil up inside me that replaces fear in record time.

"God damn it, Mom!" I roar. "I can't do this shit anymore! Do you have any idea how hard this is? To sit here and watch you waste away while I'm cleaning up your mess all the time? Working my ass off to maintain the basics around here? And yet, we're still behind on bills because you keep blowing my money on fucking booze!"

I kick the coffee table into the couch, effectively spilling all its contents. Most of the bottles roll off, creating a cacophony as they hit the floor. I turn back and yell with everything I have, releasing years of pent-up anger and resentment.

"I'm supposed to be the kid in this house, not the parent. You took that from me, and I resent you for that! Go get some help before you kill yourself. I already lost one parent. Do you really think I want to lose another?" I feel lighter, more free, with every word I spew. The chains that have kept me prisoner for so long, are breaking.

She stands there and stares, unmoving.

"What the hell happened to you, huh? What went wrong? You didn't used to be like this...until Dad left you. You used to be a good mom. Now you're just...shit."

I bend over to grasp my knees, but I'm shaking so hard that I fall to the floor. I look up into my mother's cold, lifeless eyes and see a lone tear rolling down her cheek. Mortified at the person I've become, I clasp my hand over my mouth go into hysterics. Mentally, physically, emotionally—it's too much. I was a plugged-up sink, full, on the brink of overflowing.

I cry the hardest I've ever cried in my life. I cry because even though he's not here, I know my dad would've done anything to protect me from this. I cry because there was a time where my mom—not this drunk woman in front of me—my real mom always made sure her first priority was keeping me safe and happy. And I cry because I realize that if I don't get out of this shithole, I'll be trapped in this cycle forever. And this can't be my life. I'm done trying to help her. If I can't save her, I have to save myself. I owe it to my dad to try and be happy.

FOUR

chase

It's Saturday night, and Surge is packed. I've been busting my ass for hours, and it doesn't look like it's going to slow down anytime soon. People are lined up around the bar with drink orders set to come our way. It's up to Ethan, Tamika, and me to keep up the pace. Lucky for everyone here tonight, we can multitask with the best of 'em.

As the night progresses, people start to get sloppy. Welcome to the downfall of being a bartender. We get to deal with the obnoxious drunks and, consequently, Tamika finds herself getting hit on relentlessly. She's a pro at keeping the overeager men at bay, but every once in a while, Ethan or I will step in to help her out—like tonight.

When I finish pouring a group of women their shots, I notice Christa standing near the end of the bar, scowling. I cash out their tabs, give the women their change and drinks, and head Christa's way.

"What are you doing here?" I shout over the music.

"I came to see you. You never ended up calling me like you said you would."

Christ, is she for real?

"I'm working. Can't you see that?"

"I know, but I just wanted to stop by and say hi. I didn't mean to impose…just wanted to see you."

"I can't talk right now. I have a line of people waiting."

"Can you come over later tonight after you get off so we can talk?"

"Fine, but I gotta get back to work now," I say irritably.

"Okay, just text me when you're off. I'm going bar hopping with the girls, but I should be back home by the time you're done." And with that, she turns and leaves.

After calling it a night, I end up walking away with a little over two hundred in tips. Pretty decent considering I only worked six hours. I grab my keys, clock out, and head for the back door.

Once I step outside, I pull my phone out of my pocket and notice a few missed text messages. One is from a number I don't recognize. The timestamp on it is from a couple hours ago.

Unknown: *Chase, after careful consideration I've decided to give you a shot, mainly because I need my sunglasses back, and only slightly because I actually like you. So don't get your hopes up.*

Oh, she totally likes me, she's just downplaying it. Two can play at that game. I save her number into my phone and waste no time typing out a response, hoping she's still up.

Me: *I'm glad you've finally come to your senses. I was worried that you were just going to sit back and watch the soon-to-be best thing that ever happened to you pass you by. Loving the shades btw…. I think they look better on me.*

While waiting for her response, I check my other messages. There's one from my sister, and one from Christa. Quickly, I text Megan and explain that it was a late night at work and that I'd call her tomorrow. Then I text Christa to let her know I'm on my way.

Just as the message finishes sending, my phone vibrates with another incoming text.

Mia: *Cocky much? Now come on, Chase. Is insulting me really the best way to win my affection before you even get the pleasure of taking me out on a date? And while we're on the subject, I'm certain my shades don't look that great on you…unless they're helping to conceal how utterly hideous you are.*

I laugh out loud at that one.

Me: *You're right. Where are my manners? I should wait to insult you until after our date, not before it. Pick you up at 7 on Monday night then?*

Almost instantly, I receive a response.

Mia: *Sounds good. Don't be late.*

Me: *I wouldn't dream of it.*

I slide into my sleek, black Ford Mustang and start her up. The seats are tight and firm, hugging my body in the best way. When I bought her used a couple years back, she had such low mileage, she was practically a steal. I wanted something bad ass, but still within my price range. So when my dad and I went to the dealership and saw her, I just knew she was the one. Needless to say, she's been good to me ever since.

I peel out of the parking lot and head north to Christa's place. It's always nice when I don't have to deal with the usual, downtown traffic. The drive is quiet, giving me plenty of time to think. I have to figure out how I'm going to break the news that I'm ending our fun. Can't imagine this will go over well.

Ten long minutes later, I kill the engine and give myself a couple more minutes to sort my shit out before heading up there.

When I reach her door, I knock impatiently, antsy to get this over with. After some odd seconds tick by, I try again. Still no answer. She must be passed out drunk. *Thank God, I'm off the hook.* As I'm turning to leave, I hear footsteps approaching the other side of the door. A swift click signals the unlocking of a deadbolt.

So close….

The door opens. To my surprise, I find Christa dressed in see-through lingerie. Damn.

"I've been waiting for you," she says.

There. Are. No. Words. I'm literally speechless. What did I come here to tell her again?

She smiles mischievously. "Are you going to stand there and gawk at me, or are you going to come in and keep me company?"

I'm still standing there, ogling her. She reaches up to grab the collar of my shirt and pulls me inside, closing the door behind us. She continues to walk backward—collar in hand—and pushes me down onto the couch.

She places a leg on either side of my thighs—straddling me. My palms instinctively come up behind and grab two handfuls of her ass. I start to knead her backside when she gets this epiphany look.

"I totally forgot that I bought some massage oil last week. Let me go grab it real quick. I'll be right back."

She crawls off my lap and struts out of the living room.

Once I peel my eyes from her body, I notice that her apartment is filled with mood-setting candles. The place is glowing. The weird thing is that we never do this stuff. We've never bothered to put on romantic airs for each other because we both know exactly what we are getting out of the deal—friendship and fucking. No use in trying to dress it up and turn it into something it isn't.

As my brain slowly begins to start working again, I have an epiphany myself: *Mia!*

As much as I want to fuck Christa's brains out in that skimpy little outfit, I can't. I won't. I came here for a reason. No distractions. I haul myself off the couch and start blowing all the candles out. Screaming babies invade my thoughts—my trusty and reliable method of killing untimely hard-ons. I'm happy to report it hasn't failed me yet.

Christa walks back in with the bottle of oil in her hand.

"What are you doing, Chase?"

I grab the cherry-red fleece blanket off the back of the couch. It feels like velvet between my fingertips. I rush over and bring it around her shoulders so fast you would've thought her lingerie was on fire. I bring both ends to the front and close it, shielding her body from my eyes forever. She gives me a puzzling look. I ignore it and walk us back out to the hallway.

"What the hell are you doing?" she snaps.

"Just humor me."

I take a large step back and run my hand through my hair to help formulate my thoughts. "We can't be sleeping together anymore."

There, the worst is over.

"What are you talking about? Why not?"

Clarity strikes.

"It's because of that girl, isn't it? The one from Eric's party," she accuses.

Correction—the worst is yet to come.

"Yes. I'm taking her out Monday night and she's never going to give me a chance if she knows I'm still sleeping with you."

"Since when do you care what other women think of our arrangement? It's never been an issue before, so why is it now? Besides, it's not like you have anything serious going on. You don't even know her."

"I know, but I want to make a good impression. I *need* to make a good impression. I have a gut feeling."

"You have a 'gut feeling'? Really, Chase? Enlighten me." She crosses her arms over her chest.

"I can't explain it. And even if I could, I know how far-fetched it would sound, believe me. I can't help it, I'm into her. I have no idea if it will ever become something more or not, but I haven't felt this excited about a girl in a really long time."

"Gee, thanks a lot," she says with a twinge of pain.

"I didn't mean it like that and you know it."

"Yeah, well, it still hurts."

She looks down at the ground. Exhaling, I pull her into a tight hug.

"I'm sorry that you're upset. I'm not trying to be a dick here, but you're making me feel like one."

She sighs. "It's not your fault. You told me from the start that you weren't looking for a relationship, but a part of me hoped that eventually you'd want one. Now that there's a small possibility that you may want it with her and not me, it stings."

I grimace. Although Christa isn't my girlfriend, she's still my friend, and I don't like to hurt those that I'm close to.

I release her from our embrace and cup her face in my hands. "I don't want this to ruin our friendship. That was one of my concerns early on, but you assured me that you knew what you wanted, and that didn't include a relationship. I don't want to hurt you."

Her shoulders go lax.

"I know you never meant to hurt me. But having said that, I need some space."

She fidgets in contemplation. "I think you should go," she says definitively.

This is how we are—blunt and honest. Unlikely to hold grudges. When I argue with her, it's like having an argument with Eric; we say what we need to say, then it's done. In my experience, most women aren't like that. They argue everything to death, throw it back in your face, and hold it over your head for the next ten years of your life.

Christa walks into the apartment, then turns back around to face me. "I really hope you know what you're doing."

"Goodnight, Christa."

The door starts to close, but I brace my hand against it and lean forward. "For the record, the lingerie is a ten."

The tiniest of smiles appears. "Eat your heart out."

Knowing all too well that I deserve that comment, I smile and push myself off the doorframe. My mood is slightly lifted. I hope Christa and I can work things out down the road. She really is a cool girl to hang with, but now that I've cut ties with her sexually, my conscious is clear when it comes to a certain girl whose text messages I can't get out of my head. Monday night can't come soon enough.

FIVE

a m e l i a

Procrastination is one vicious bitch. It's officially Monday morning and I still haven't unpacked. I also haven't responded to any of Mom's messages from Saturday morning, either. If I ignore her, then I can pretend the problem will go away on its own. Duck and dodge: that's my motto. If a tornado is heading your way, you wouldn't prance into it, arms wide open, would you? No. You duck and take cover. Or, if you're feeling especially zealous, you run like hell.

Since I spent the majority of my weekend watching old movies with Raven and shamelessly stuffing my face with pizza and beer, I decide it's time to start being productive. Raven already left for class over an hour ago, so she's one step ahead of me in that department.

I grab my phone off the nightstand and leisurely stroll across the hall into her room to use her stereo. If I'm going to do mind-numbing, back-breaking labor (i.e., unpacking), then I'm at least going to listen to some good tunes to make it more bearable.

Music has always been a huge part of my life. I'd go as far to say that it's essential to extending the human lifespan. Can you honestly imagine a world without music? I think our souls would wither away and die. I know mine would.

Growing up, Dad used to have a record player in our living room. It sat next to an old bookcase that housed his collection of vinyls. He played a lot of The Beatles, Queen, and The Clash—some of his favorites. Subsequently, they became my favorites. He used to come home from work, throw a record on, and spin me around the living room before bedtime.

Eventually, that record player stopped working, and my mom bought a stereo. Dad was against that. He always believed that vinyl sounded better, but he couldn't say no to Mom. The record player sat in the basement collecting dust until he left. Mom eventually threw it out because it reminded her too much of him. She also got rid of his collection, but not before I could snag one very important album off that shelf—Pink Floyd's *The Dark Side of the Moon*. That record is so valuable to me that—instead of hiding it in my house and running the risk of my mom finding it—I asked Hadley to keep it safe at her place. Now, that beloved record sits in one of those unopened boxes across the hall.

I queue up some Beastie Boys to kickstart the task, and I drop to my knees and begin peeling the boxes open, one by one. I focus on hanging up all of my clothes and organizing the few pairs of shoes I was able to bring.

After emptying every last box, I decide to shower and run to the mall to buy a new outfit for my date tonight. I didn't bother to bring any of my fancy clothes to Austin; it didn't make any sense to when I hardly ever wear them. Instead, I planned on doing some shopping after I settled in and lined up some job interviews. Looking back, I should've packed them, but the possibility of going out on a date with someone had never crossed my mind. Not this soon, anyway.

By the time I get back to the apartment, Raven's all done with her classes for the day. I set my shopping bags down on the dining room table and kick off my shoes. Snatching the bags off the table, I traipse down the hallway toward her room. Her door is partially open; she's sitting cross-legged on her bed, doing homework. I can feel the intensity of the study zone.

Sensing my presence, she looks up from her textbook and slides her reading glasses onto her head. "Ooh, what'd you g—wait a minute, you went shopping without me?"

"Sorry, but you were in class and I didn't want to wait until the last minute," I shrug.

"It's not last minute." She glances down at her phone. "Your date is still three hours away. You couldn't wait for me to get home?"

"No, I was too excited. Happy?"

"Happy that you copped to the truth? Yes. Happy that you still went shopping without me? Uh...no, bitch. Now show me what you bought," she huffs.

I plaster on the biggest smile—my way of calling a truce. My mom used to say that if you have a girlfriend who makes people question your sexuality on a daily basis, that one's a keeper. Turns out, she was right. I'm sure handfuls of people out there assume we're lesbians—Eric being one of them. *He wishes.* Can't say he doesn't dream big.

Knowing exactly what my scorned lover needs in order to feel better, I reach down and pull the box of shoes out of the bag. I remove the lid and crawl onto her bed. Situating myself up on my knees, I straddle her and present the box.

She lights up, eagerly snatching it out of my hands. She pushes me backward. I flop against the bed, laughing. She examines the boots lovingly. "Oh, my God! I'm totally borrowing these. You are going to look so freaking hot tonight!"

"You think so?" I ask, propping myself up on my elbows.

She gives me a don't-be-ridiculous look. "I know so. Chase better not screw this up."

God bless girlfriends who lift you up and champion you.

"If you want, I have some earrings that would go really well with these. You should wear them."

"I'd love to, thank you. Also, I have a favor to ask."

She sets the boots down and gives me her full attention. "What's up?"

"Can you please do my hair and give me those loose curls? You know, the ones that will make him visualize fisting my hair in his hand and giving it a nice pull," I say with a wink.

"Absolutely." She smirks.

Three hours later, I'm dressed and ready. I feel confident and sexy, but my nerves have spiked. *When was the last time I went out on a date?* My palms are clammy and my heart is in my throat.

My hair is curled to perfection and pinned back on one side. The chandelier earrings look great with the outfit, and after applying and reapplying my makeup fifteen trillion times, I finally settled on charcoal eye shadow. It gives my eyes a smoky, heated look. Now if I could only stop sweating. *Ugh, I hate dating. Why the hell did I agree to this?*

"You look gorgeous. Stop fidgeting so much," Raven scolds, running her fingers through my curls, putting the finishing touches on me.

"I can't help it. I'm nervous."

"He's going to be here any minute. Pull it together. The last thing you want is to look like Ben Stiller when he went on that dinner date with Jennifer Aniston in *Along Came Polly*. That was just gross."

Great. That's a visual I didn't need in my head. A very sweaty Ben Stiller with irritable bowel syndrome who later practically shits himself to death at her place afterward. *Awesome.*

I jog out of the bathroom and into the kitchen to open the freezer and lift my arms up to air out my pits, representing the epitome of class and sexiness in the name of every woman out there. Just when I feel like my nerves are under control, there's a knock at the door.

Oh God, he's here. How did he get past the gate? Do I look sexy? I'm not sure I feel sexy. Maybe his version of sexy and mine are totally different. What if he tries to kiss me tonight? Do I want to be kissed? I don't want to come off too easy. What if the only reason he's interested in me is because he thinks I'm easy? Oh fuck off, Mia!

I briskly close the freezer door and block out the rambling. Raven emerges from the hallway and gives me two thumbs up.

"Ready?" she mouths.

I take a deep breath and nod.

She peeks through the peephole and opens the door.

"Hey, Raven," I hear him say.

"Hey, yourself," she greets.

She gives him a swift one-arm hug, then moves aside to let him in the apartment. He steps inside and a gorgeous bouquet of deep red calla lilies captures my attention. *He bought me flowers?*

Chase is dressed in black dress pants, black dress shoes, and a royal blue button-down that's rolled up to his elbows. The color in his tats pops against the shirt, as I'm sure his eyes would if he weren't wearing my Aviators. I suddenly feel underdressed. *Shit, so much for playing it safe.* He looks ruggedly handsome.

"Here, I can take those," Raven offers, motioning to the flowers. Chase doesn't catch her offer, or if he does, he isn't acknowledging it. He's too busy staring at me. He tilts my sunglasses just below his eyes and his gaze sweeps my body from head to toe. His attention makes me nervous—again.

Raven takes the flowers and makes her way past me. I hear her grab a vase from the cupboard and turn on the faucet.

Chase saunters toward me until there's less than a foot between us. He lifts my sunglasses onto his head and holds me with his gaze. The intensity makes me feel uneasy, yet I can't look away. I wouldn't dare. I don't know if I'll get beyond a first date, so I'm going to soak it up. After all, it's not very often someone can make me feel this way.

"You look stunning," he praises, only amplifying that feeling.

"I feel underdressed," I blurt out.

I internally face-palm myself. *Way to ruin the moment.*

His lips curve up into a slow smile, making my heart skip a beat or two. "You aren't," he assures me. "I overdid it on purpose because I want you to feel special tonight—but only tonight. This shit wears off tomorrow," he jokes.

Thank God. That comment puts me at ease.

"Shall we?" he offers his hand.

We say our goodbyes to Raven and head out the door.

"Have her back by eleven!" she yells.

Laughing, we make our way down to his car. He stops on the passenger's side to open my door. I slide in and meet the warm leather; my body immediately sticks to the seat. He walks around to his side and climbs in. The engine roars to life, and before I've even managed to get my seatbelt on, we're off.

"So where are we headed?" I ask.

"To one of my favorite restaurants. They serve really good Mediterranean food and they have a nice patio area. I hope you're okay with that."

"Sounds great."

He looks young and edgy as he shifts the car into gear, taking the on-ramp. He has one hand placed on the steering wheel and he's wearing my sunglasses again. There's a little bit of sunlight left, but it's quickly fading. The sky is filled with vivid shades of fuchsia, red, and orange. All of the colors look like they're melting together, like something you'd see in a painting.

"Thank you for the flowers, by the way. They're beautiful."

"This is the part where I'm supposed to pull out another cheesy line and tell you that you are far more beautiful, huh?"

"No," I say adamantly. "Don't ever say something you don't mean. Just be real. I'll value your honesty far more than any compliment you could sling my way."

I think about that statement and then realize it's only a half-truth. "Now having said that, if you feel the need to give me a compliment, I'm not opposed to that either," I tease.

He laughs. "Well, in that case, you are far more beautiful than those flowers...but they smell better."

I let out a hearty laugh.

He grins and looks back and forth between the road and me. "What? You think I'm joking?"

That makes me laugh even harder. I've never met anyone so charming and so offensive at the same time. It's a gift—the way he can work both traits to his advantage. He reaches over and uses the backs of his knuckles to lightly brush my cheek. My breath catches and I instantly stop laughing. Suddenly, this car feels a hell of a lot smaller. He proceeds to run a single finger over my bare shoulder, making me shiver.

"I dig this look on you."

I clear my throat, feeling slightly self-conscious, but more turned on than anything else.

"You don't look so bad yourself."

"Good to know."

I try to distract myself from the sexual tension by looking out the window and enjoying the view. I love how the weather is warm and the trees are still green in October. I glance at all of the overpasses that used to be intimidating. I think about how my life has changed so drastically. Last week, I was living in the same small town I'd always known, working the same two jobs with the same small community of people, just traveling through life, day in and day out.

Now, I've moved on to a much bigger city where I know virtually *no one*. I mean, other than Raven and Eric, I have no one else. The thought is both scary and invigorating.

I sneak a peek at Chase again and think about how nice it is to sit here, silently. I don't feel pressured to carry on a conversation. I'm sure with any other first date, this would be incredibly awkward. But with him, it feels natural, comfortable. I feel like I can be myself and not worry about presenting some unrealistic, "acceptable" version of who I am.

When we arrive at Fino, Chase walks around the vehicle to open my door. I step out, and he gently places his hand on the middle of my back, leading me inside. The gesture makes me feel exceptional. I have to bite my lip to keep a huge smile from breaking out. The last thing I want is to look like some overeager, lovestruck teenager.

Too late for that.

We're instantly greeted by the hostess and we follow her to a cozy table for two. The restaurant has a romantic feel to it with its earthy color tones. We take our seats, grab the menus, and survey our options.

"I take it you've never been here before?" Chase asks.

I shake my head.

"Well, I hope you like it. Order whatever you want. If you need any suggestions, just let me know."

"I will. Thank you."

When the server comes up to our table, Chase orders a beer. I choose to stick with water.

"You sure you don't want a drink?" he checks.

"No, I had more than my fair share of beer and pizza this past weekend."

"Beer and pizza, huh? Sounds like the breakfast of champions."

"Oh, it was, believe me. And lunch. And dinner."

"Now that's a real woman—someone who can actually eat a meal and enjoy something more than a salad. I fully support your healthy eating habits," he winks.

My entire face flushes, and I turn my attention back to the menu. I wish I'd remembered to bring a pair of sunglasses, because, my God, if this isn't a sunglasses moment, I don't know what is. *Don't be awkward and weird, Mia. He'll sense it.*

When our waiter returns with our drinks, we order dinner. I end up going with the pan-seared salmon and Chase orders the Pacific Gulf shrimp. We hand the menus back and Chase folds his arms over the table, focusing his attention on me. It appears the classic getting-to-know-you inquisition is upon us.

"How's Austin treating you so far?"

I smile, relieved. "I love it. It's so nice to be back. Only this time, I get to stay."

"So you're staying here indefinitely?"

"Yeah, for now. I have nowhere else to go. I have some money saved up, but not enough to make it on my own, unfortunately."

"You don't like sharing a place with Raven?" he asks.

"No, it's not that. I just don't like depending on other people when I've been taking care of myself for so long. In a way, moving down here is taking a step back. I had to swallow some pride, which I hate doing."

"Me too," he sympathizes. "If you don't mind me asking, why'd you leave home?"

I suck in a sharp breath and try to think of a way to skirt around the issue.

"Um, my mom and I haven't been getting along too well. We had an argument, and she needed some space. So I packed my bags and drove ten hours to give her that space, so she could think long and hard about her actions. She'd tell you that I'm being dramatic, but I choose to think of myself as an over-achieving daughter," I joke.

"Life's all about perspective," he says instantly.

I smile and feel some of the tension leave my body. "Enough about me, what's your family like? Do have any siblings?"

He leans back in his chair and relaxes. "I do. I have an older sister. She and I are extremely close when she isn't blowing up my phone and nagging me on a daily basis. She's twenty-eight—two years older than me—and she lives with her husband in North Austin. What about you? Any siblings?"

I shake my head. "Nope, I'm your stereotypical only child who hates to share."

He leans forward again, keeping his eyes trained on mine. "Can I tell you a secret? I'm glad you don't like to share, because I don't either."

Holy shit.

"What about your parents?" I quickly ask, throwing the spotlight back on him.

"My dad owns a construction company and my mom teaches fourth grade. They're both still happily married."

"That's awesome. I admire couples who can stay happily married for that long."

"Are your parents divorced?"

"Yeah, they divorced when I was little and my dad moved down here a few years after that. Neither one of them ever remarried, though. My dad passed away a couple years ago, and it's been my mom and I ever since."

"I'm really sorry about your dad," he says. "What happened?"

"He died in a car accident on his way home from work one night. Drunk driver," I mutter dejectedly.

This is a sore spot. I don't like to talk about my dad. The fact that his death was caused by a drunk driver, and my mother is a raging alcoholic, only pours salt into the wound. Even though she was having problems long before he died, I only grew to resent her more after he was killed. If she wasn't so selfish, my father would have never left her and moved here. He'd probably still be alive, and I would've had a chance at a normal childhood. But then, a part of me feels incredibly guilty for feeling that way about my own mother. It's so emotionally draining to love a parent with all your heart, and yet, completely despise them for who they are. It's a vicious cycle that gnaws away at you like a chronic illness.

Thankfully, the food arrives in perfect time. Everything smells delicious and is cooked to perfection. We dig in.

"How does everything taste?" he asks.

"Absolutely delicious. Want some?" I offer.

He shakes his head. "No, thank you. You?"

"Yeah, actually, I'll try a bite if you're willing to share."

"No way. I was only trying to be polite."

I lean forward, set my forearm on the table, and lower my voice. "Give me a bite of that shrimp, you dirty whore."

He laughs. "Oh, really? You want some of this, do you?" The way he says that, it's hard to tell whether he means the shrimp or himself.

I narrow my eyes and sit back. "You know, on second thought, changed my mind. It doesn't really look all that appetizing, after all."

His gaze intensifies, releasing a hunger that makes him look dangerous. He's challenging me, daring me. I feel my body respond. I reach for my glass of water and take a few sips to try and cool myself down from the inside out—a feeble attempt. Instead, I refocus all my attention on my dinner, avoiding his gaze like the plague. At this rate, it's going to be a long night.

SIX

c h a s e

Jesus. I'm in a restaurant, on a date with a beautiful woman, having good conversation, but all I can seem to think about is bending her over this table and fucking her until she can't see straight. She wants it, too. I can see it in her eyes. She's looking at me like she wants me to ravage her body, right here, right now.

Get it under control, dude.

I practically inhale my food and signal for our check so we can get out of here. There's somewhere I want to take her after this, and for once, the backseat of my car is not what I have in mind. I sign the receipt, leave a generous tip, and waste no time leaving.

"Where are we going?" she asks, once we've made it to the car.

"It's a surprise. Just relax and enjoy the ride."

I drive us into downtown with the windows down. It's gotten a little cooler out, but I think it's safe to assume the breeze feels nice for both of us. Many of the restaurants and bars are lit up with

Christmas lights, making the drive that much more enjoyable. This is an Austin thing. They leave up lights all year 'round. Unless you live here, you wouldn't understand how appropriate of a thing that is to do for Austin's vibe. We pass multiple food carts that serve some of the most amazing hangover food you'll ever eat, and I mentally make a note to bring Mia here soon.

Fifteen minutes later, we reach our destination. I turn off the car, grab the cooler from the back seat, and step out. She follows. When she closes the door, I shoot her a nervous glance over the top of my car. I hope she likes what I have planned.

"Mini-golf?" she asks, amused.

"Damn right, mini-golf," I defend.

"What's in the cooler?"

"Beer. It's BYOB. No better way to have some fun than to drink booze and get your ass kicked in a round of mini-golf. See how that works?"

She shakes her head and smiles. "You know, you continue to surprise me."

"Good. Keep trying to figure me out. It's far more entertaining when you're wrong. Plus, mystery keeps romance alive, and I plan on having this thing between us go on for a little while longer, like, maybe another week or so."

"You're shameless," she muses.

"Don't you ever forget it."

After paying, we each pick out our clubs and the color of ball we want. I choose red, she chooses purple. We walk to the first hole. I set the cooler down and fetch two cold cans of beer and pass one to

Mia. It's dark out now, but the course is lit up nicely. There are only two other groups here, but they're quite a ways ahead of us, so we won't have to worry about feeling rushed.

"Okay, so here's how this is going to work. We will take turns, and for every time that we miss a shot, the other one gets to ask a question. No more heavy stuff. Just fun, random facts."

"I like that a lot. You get to go first because I want to ask the first question. Here, I'll hold your beer while you take your shot." She sticks her club under her elbow and holds out her hand.

I place my beer in her hand, line up the ball, and take a swing. Miss.

"What's your favorite movie?" she asks.

"*The Shawshank Redemption.* Your turn."

She hands me the beers and lines herself up. She takes her shot and misses.

"What did you want to be when you were a kid?"

"A marine biologist. Honestly, when it came down to it, I just wanted to see the ocean and swim with a dolphin." She laughs.

I take the next shot and make it. She follows. Misses.

"What's your favorite band?"

She looks at me like I just asked her to solve a physics problem.

"Um...are you crazy? I have a new favorite band every five minutes. I could never choose just one. It all depends on my mood. I do have a favorite album. Does that count?"

"Yeah, that works."

"*The Dark Side of the Moon* by Pink Floyd is easily one of the greatest albums ever made."

"That's a great one," I agree. "You have excellent taste, but I can't say that I'm surprised."

"Why, thank you," she says coyly.

We continue playing for an hour or so, and all too soon, we are coming up on the last hole. By this point, we both realized how much we suck at mini-golf. I can't be too upset about that, though, because it gave us numerous chances to find out more information about each other.

She learned that my favorite color is blue, my favorite flavor of ice cream is mint chocolate chip, and I had my first real kiss when I was fourteen. She asked about the scar above my left eyebrow, which happened when I was seven. I was jumping on our couch and fell off. My face hit the corner of our coffee table just right, which resulted in a trip to the hospital for five stitches. Mom was pissed.

As for Mia: I know that she has an intense, love-hate relationship with coffee, she's dying to travel to Australia, and perhaps, most importantly, if she could have one superpower, she would want to move things with her mind. *Epic.*

She filled me in on what her hometown was like. Told me the town has a strong Swedish heritage (which, apparently, is a big deal in Lindsborg) and the people are friendly. She said the town itself wasn't a bad place to be raised—more like it was the house she was raised in—but she didn't go into any detail. She also filled me in on a couple of her crazy adventures with Hadley—including a steamy kiss they shared together, which instantly got my mind wandering. I have no doubt she did that on purpose to fuck up my game. And damn it, it worked.

Even though we're both shitty golfers, she's technically winning. So, I decide to switch things up. That way, no matter what happens, I'll come out ahead.

"Okay, so since this is the last hole, I'm raising the stakes. Sound good?"

She looks at me skeptically but nods.

"If I can make this a hole-in-one, I get to kiss you. Deal?"

She crosses her arms over her chest. "And if I make it in one shot, what do I get?"

"Well, I'm inclined to say that you would have the rare and great opportunity to kiss me, but I'll be nice and let you pick your own prize."

"Hmm," she taps her index finger against her lips. "How about if I make it, then I get to drive your precious Mustang back home?"

No fucking way.

Absolutely not.

Over my dead body.

"Deal. Shake on it." I stick out my hand, resentful. She grabs it and gives me a firm shake like when we first met. I'm not that worried because the chances of her actually making this are slim. Plus, I'm assuming she doesn't know how to drive a stick shift.

She sets her ball down and steps back to the side, then bends her body slightly and lines up her club, concentrating on the task. I take the moment to check out her ass in those jeans. *Perfection.* She takes a few deep breaths and lightly rocks the club back and forth. She pulls back and hits the ball with quite a bit of force, but she has to because there's a large (mini) hill. The ball hurdles over the hill but goes over and down the opposite side, hitting the ledge.

"That's ridiculous!"

The pouty look on her face is so pathetic, I can't help but gloat. I casually stroll to where she was standing and set my ball down. I turn to look at her real quick. "Now remember, if I make this, I get to kiss you. No going back on your word just because you suck."

She rolls her eyes. "Fine."

I look down at the ball and concentrate on making this shot. It's lined up perfectly, and I'm preparing to take my swing. At the last second, I switch it up and start moving quickly toward the hole, using the club to slide the ball the entire way down.

"Hey, that's cheating!" Mia shouts.

I manage to get it over the hill and sink it. I spin around and point my club in her direction.

"That, my lovely Mia, is called a hole-in-one. I do believe you owe me a kiss."

"No way. I'm not kissing you after that poor excuse for a shot."

"Face the facts, you lost that bet and it's time for you to pay up."

"If you can cheat to win, then I can cheat to get out of the bet."

"On what grounds?"

"On the grounds that you cheated!"

"First you reject me, then you defame my character? How far will you go?"

"It's not a defamation of character if it's true."

I contemplate how I'm going to be able to bargain a kiss out of this girl. Suddenly, inspiration strikes.

"I'll tell you what, because I want that kiss so badly, I'll let you drive my Mustang home regardless of the fact that you lost."

She opens her mouth to give me a response but then quickly snaps it shut. A moment or two goes by, and she's still standing there. I slowly make my way toward her despite her defensive stance. As I approach, she backs up. I bring the club around her back and use it to pull her body flush against mine.

We're standing so close that I can feel her breath against the front of my throat. I place my hand on the side of her neck, just below her ear. I lean in, my face mere centimeters from hers, and bring my mouth to her earlobe. I gently tug it in between my teeth and give it a playful nip. Her breathing becomes shallow, and it only winds me up more. I want to make this woman completely fall apart in my arms. I exhale directly into her ear and she begins to sway. I drop the club and wrap my other arm around her back.

I pull my head back just a fraction so I can look into her eyes.

"Admit it, you wanted me to make the shot."

She tenses up. My hand moves from her neck down to grip her hip. Her eyes look like hot, hazel lava, like she's melting away and burning with desire. I do this to her. I make her feel this way. And when the time comes to have her in my bed, I'll give her the hardest eruption she's ever had.

I swiftly move in and fuse my mouth to hers before it's too late. It only takes her a moment to process, and she closes her eyes and reciprocates. It starts out slow and gentle but quickly escalates to passionate and frenzied. Her lips are as soft as satin. My heart is pounding so hard; I can feel the throbbing on my lips as I kiss her.

My fingers slide up the back of her neck and fist her hair, holding her face to mine. She tastes like beer, but her kisses are far more intoxicating than the alcohol.

She places her hands on either side of my face and our bodies bind together like one. It's a good thing we're the only ones here, because with the way we're kissing, it's not suitable for children...or uptight prudes. It's taking everything I have not to pick her up and walk her to my car.

When we finally get so low on oxygen, or so high on each other that we're lightheaded, we break the kiss. I rest my forehead against hers and take a moment to calm down and listen to our accelerated breathing. That's twice in one hour that this girl has sent me into a tailspin of arousal.

"That was incredible," I say.

"Yeah, it was all right, I guess. A little anti-climactic after waiting for you to take the final shot, but whatever," she pants.

I throw my head back and laugh. God this woman slays me. Kissing her on the lips once more, I release her and reach down to pick up the cooler.

"Come on, let's get the hell out of here."

"Are you taking me back to my place?"

"Do you want to go back to your place?" I freeze, holding my breath. *Say no.*

"Not really. I don't care where we go, but I'm not ready to go back yet."

"Good, because I was going to take you back to my place for a bit."

She places her hands on her hips. "Is that so?"

"Don't worry. I told you before that I'd be on my best behavior, and I meant it."

She gives me a dubious look.

"Fine, maybe not my very best behavior, but it certainly won't be my worst. Now let's get out of here." I throw my arm around the back of her neck and pull her into me. As much as I hate doing the whole girlfriend thing, I must admit, Mia's growing on me.

SEVEN

a m e l i a

Chase kept his word. We went back to his place last night, cuddled up on the couch, and "watched" a movie. Translation: we kissed until our lips were chapped, making us both all hot and bothered. He ended up dropping me back off at my place a little after midnight. He walked me to the door and kissed me goodnight like a perfect gentleman. We both agreed that we wanted to go out again this weekend, but he said that he'd have to check his work schedule and get back to me. I hope that isn't guy code for: I had a great time with you last night, but don't count on me calling.

I throw the covers back and hop out of bed, then walk out to the kitchen to brew a pot of coffee.

A couple minutes later, Raven comes strolling out with wet hair, wearing only a towel around her torso. "Good morning," she beams.

"Morning. Coffee?"

"Yes, please." She takes a seat on one of the bar stools.

I grab a mug from the cupboard and pour her a hot cup. Sliding her the mug, I reach for another one and pour some for myself. I add a couple spoonfuls of sugar and walk around the center island to take the seat next to her.

"So...how did it go last night?" she asks, eager for information.

"Oh, my God, Rave, I had so much fun. He's so different from what I was expecting. He's sweet and charming and funny, but he's also got just the right amount of bad boy in him, too," I gush.

"Tell me everything," she demands.

"Well, first he took me out to dinner and then we went mini-golfing."

"Mini-golfing?"

"That was my reaction, too. But it was actually a lot of fun."

"You know what, now that I think about it, that has Chase written all over it. But anyways, continue." She waves her hand, prompting me.

"To sum it up, we ended up back at his place, but we kept things PG."

"No hookup?"

I shake my head. "No hookup."

"Good kisser?"

"*Fantastic.*"

I proceed to give her all the deets when, suddenly, my phone starts buzzing.

"Shit, that's my mom."

"Are you going to answer it?"

"No, I'll let it go to voicemail and call her back later."

"You know you can't ignore her forever, Mia."

"I know, I know," I say, exasperated.

"I'm serious. Get it over with. Rip the bandage off. Maybe if you tell her you're okay, and let her know you need some space, she'll leave you alone."

"Believe me, I wish it were that easy."

Raven forces a small smile and drops it. We continue to sip our coffee in awkward silence. The only sound in the apartment is the ticking coming from the clock on the wall.

I really do wish it were that simple. I wish my mom and I could work things out, but the bottom line is, you can't save someone who doesn't want to be saved.

Apparently, despite my best efforts, you can't outrun your past, either. No matter how far you go, and how fast you run, your problems will eventually catch up with you. The only way I'm truly going to move past all this, is by facing the music and calling my mother back. It's certainly better than putting it off and having an uneasy feeling growing in the pit of my stomach all day.

Raven clears her throat. "I've got to go get ready for class."

"What are your plans for tonight?"

"I have to work," she says apologetically.

"No worries. I have stuff I should get done today. I need to start looking for a job and run a few errands."

"I can see if the restaurant is hiring. I'm sure if there's a spot open, my parents would hire you in a heartbeat," she offers.

"I appreciate that, but you've done enough for me already. I think I'm just going to apply to a few steakhouses around the area. If I have trouble finding something on my own, then maybe I'll get back to you on that offer."

"Okay, let me know if you change your mind," she says, standing up. She walks around the center island, rinses out her mug, and puts it in the dishwasher.

"Hey, Rave?"

She looks up expectantly.

"Yeah?"

"Thanks again for the talk. As much as I don't want to admit it, I know you're right."

Her eyes soften. "You're welcome."

She starts walking out of the kitchen but turns back around. "Oh, before I forget, ACL going on at Zilker Park this weekend if you're interested. Eric and I got tickets for everyone ahead of time, but one of our friends backed out last minute, so there's an extra ticket up for grabs if you want it. I also may happen to know something about Chase having a ticket of his own," she hints.

My heart jumps at the idea. Austin City Limits is an extremely popular music festival that goes on for a couple weekends in the fall. It's a big deal, and it's the first time I've ever been able to go. Knowing Chase will be there, too, is like the icing on one very delectable cake. Raven couldn't have made a better sale if she was an ice water saleswoman in the Mojave at high noon.

I give her a slow smile. "I adore you."

"I'll take that as a yes." She spins on a heel and leaves to finish getting ready.

• • •

"Mom, for the last time, I'm not coming back and I'm not giving you any more money."

I finally worked up the courage to call, waiting for Raven leave for class. It's close to twelve, which means my mom has already started drinking, but she isn't incoherent and bitchy yet. This is a calculated move—to call her back now instead of waiting until later in the day. She's easier to deal with. The reason she called me earlier was to remind me about the house payment that's due on the first. Figures. This woman usually can't remember jack shit—my birthday, graduation—but she never fails to remember when I'm supposed to pay the house bill.

"Why not? Do you not care about keeping a roof over our heads?"

"I don't live there anymore."

"Well, what about keeping a roof over my head? Do you not care about me anymore? You think you're too good for this place now, is that it?"

I roll my eyes and bite my tongue. Typical Mom. If she isn't shitting on me, then she's guilt tripping me.

"No, Mom, that's not it. I told you I was done. I wasn't kidding when I said that."

"Oh, that's bullshit and you know it. You can't just up and move your entire life somewhere. You have responsibilities. You have bills to pay."

I take a calming breath and try not to let her succeed with her guilt tripping schemes. She knows exactly which buttons to push. I'm tired of always feeling guilty for her fuckups.

I immediately recall the last conversation I had with my therapist before I left home. She told me I had to let go and try to get my mom professional help. According to her, it isn't my responsibility to keep my mom above water. She warned me that my mom would probably have to hit rock bottom before she gets better. Apparently, we're still in the seemingly never-ending spiral stage, and she hasn't hit her bottom yet.

"Mom, I'm cutting you off financially. I *have* cut you off financially. I'm not going back on my word. You need help and I need a chance to live my life."

I sit down on the edge of my bed and take another deep breath before continuing. It's hard for me to say no to her, and, to be honest, I'm still learning and coaching myself as I go.

"I love you, but you need help that I'm not able to give. By sticking around and taking care of you, I'm only enabling you to keep drinking. I can't be your crutch anymore."

"Fine, we'll just see how you feel about all of this when I lose the house. I'll be on the streets and you'll have no place to come back to when things go wrong down there in good ol' Oklahoma."

Her words burn me like acid.

"Texas, Mom. I'm in Texas."

"Whatever. Don't even think about calling me for help. You're on your own now."

"Always have been, always will be," I counter.

She hangs up. I let out a pained breath and lay back on my bed to stare at the ceiling. Even though I'm so far away, it feels as if I'm back there. And, as horrible as this sounds, I just wish she would find someone to take care of her so that she doesn't have to be my problem anymore. She's become nothing but a financial burden over the years, and I've given up a lot, especially to have it thrown back in my face.

Instead of getting upset over something I can't control, I decide to go for a run to let off some steam. I throw my hair into a ponytail and change into my yoga pants, a tank, and running shoes. I reach for my headphones on the nightstand, plug them into my phone, and select "Plan B" by Mutemath to block out my thoughts.

After my run and a nice cold shower, I ran some errands—went to the post office, the bank, and even picked up some applications from a few places nearby that are in need of servers. I also did the one thing that I avoid till the very last second—grocery shopping. Seriously, I'd rather call my mom and talk to her for an hour. As always, I ended up buying a bunch of food that looked really good at the time, but I know I won't eat later.

I open the trunk and glance around. Ah, the game of *how the hell am I going to carry all this stuff up to my apartment in one trip?* has begun. Something has to give because there's no way I'm making two trips. I grab as many bags as I can manage before I feel like Macaulay Culkin in *Home Alone* when he's walking home and all those groceries collapse. I turn in the general direction of the apartment with veins popping out from both forearms—more proof of my inherent sexiness.

"Need some help with those?" a smooth voice asks from behind me.

I know that voice. *Chase.*

I turn around. He's standing there, watching me with a gleam in his eye. He's leaning against his car with his arms crossed over his chest and his feet crossed at the ankles. He's dressed in dark jeans and a black T-shirt, his face is clean-shaven today. He looks devastatingly gorgeous. It's *so* uncharacteristic. I want to drop all these bags on the ground and forcefully kiss him—like a dramatic scene out of a movie. But I choose to stand here and give him a hard time, instead.

"Look at that, you've only had one date with me and already you're a stage-five clinger."

"What can I say? Just can't help myself when it comes to you."

That is such a cheesy line, but unfortunately, it's working. And the way he's standing there with his arms crossed, challenging me with those stormy eyes, it pisses me off because it makes my heart palpitate. I secretly love it, even though I'm going to repeatedly tell myself that I don't.

"How long have you been standing there? What are you doing here? And how did you get past the gate?"

"I've only been here a couple minutes and I used the code to get in. Raven gave it to me a few months back. I knocked on the door but no one was home. I was just getting into my car to leave when I saw you pull in. Talk about perfect timing. It's as if fate is trying to tell us something, don't you think?"

"Are you actually going to help me carry these up, or are you just going to stand there and listen to the sound of your voice?" I ask.

"I suppose I could help you out, but not without something in return." He comes up, grabs my face, and lays a kiss on me.

"There," he says, satisfied. "Now I'll help."

Chase follows me upstairs with the majority of the groceries, and I unlock the door to let him in. He goes to the kitchen and sets everything on the counter. I follow with the bag I'm holding. He eyes the vase of calla lilies that are on display, and I can sense his pride.

We start taking everything out of the bags, and I'm all too aware of his presence. Every now and then, our arms lightly brush up against each other's and my heart skips at the contact. He's fighting back a smile, like he knows exactly what I'm feeling right now. I'm starting to become a nervous wreck. I can't concentrate when he's in my personal space like this.

"Go ahead and make yourself comfortable while I put these away," I say, aiming to put a little distance between us. I desperately want to keep my cool, or at least salvage what's left of it.

He nods and walks over to the couch, taking a seat.

"Where's Raven?"

"She's working."

"So you're telling me that we have the entire place to ourselves?"

"Yes, and don't even think about it," I warn.

He holds up both of his hands like I just pulled a gun on him. "Just kidding. I wouldn't try anything…unless you were open to it."

"I appreciate that. Now why are you here again?"

"I came by to give your sunglasses back because I forgot, again, last night when I dropped you off. Plus, I checked both of my schedules and I wanted to set our second date."

He could've texted me to set the second date, and he could've waited until he saw me to give me my sunglasses back. He's here because he wants to see me, but he doesn't want me to think he's desperate. I lean over to put the milk on the bottom shelf of the fridge and release a big smile where he can't see. He isn't the only one who's suffering from a severe case of self-protection. Just then, the conversation I had with Raven this morning comes floating back.

"Speaking of our second date, Raven said ACL is going on this weekend. She and Eric will both be there on Saturday…and so will I. Are you interested?" I'm feeling him out. Even though I know he already has a ticket, I don't want him to feel obligated to hang out with me if he'd rather be with his friends.

Those dimples appear on his cheeks again. He looks far more young and innocent now that he's shaved off his facial hair. He looks great either way, but I almost prefer him with some scruff.

"That's funny because I was just going to ask if you wanted to go with me. I don't normally get the music festivals off, but I got lucky this year."

I hits me that I don't even know what he does for a living. I know it will only be our second date, but that's usually something that's covered on a first. *How did I miss that?* I mentally kick myself.

"Where do you work, anyway?" I ask curiously.

"I'm a carpenter for my dad's furniture company. I also bartend at Surge on the side."

I've heard about Surge. Supposedly, it's quite the hot spot downtown, but it's more of an upscale bar, less of a dive. That tells me right off the bat it probably won't appeal to my tastes.

"Why'd you choose to work for your dad's company? Did you feel pressured to work for the family business or something?"

"No, not really. My dad and I were always building things together when I was a kid, and I just seem to have a knack for it," he shrugs. "Mostly, I enjoy it. When I'm working on something, I don't worry about anything else that's going on. It clears my head and puts me at ease. You know how some people cook, clean, or exercise to get that feeling?"

I nod.

He smiles and points to himself. "This guy likes to build shit."

"What kind of shit?"

"Anything inside of a house, but mainly furniture."

"Seriously? You can furnish a house?" I ask, surprised. "That's impressive. Wish I could do something like that."

"I'll teach you how sometime."

The thought of learning something new and getting to see Chase in his element excites me. I want to see what he can do with what he considers his passion.

"I'd really like that."

Once I finish putting everything away, I receive a text from Hadley asking me if it's a good time to call.

"Are you staying for a while?" I ask.

"Sorry, can't. I gotta work at the bar tonight. That's one of the reasons why I stopped by. I'll be busy this week and I won't get to see you again until Saturday."

It bums me out that I won't be able to see him anymore this week, but I get that he's busy. He sets my sunglasses down on the coffee table and stands, walking toward me. My heart rate spikes. He reaches out and cups my face in his hands and brings me up on my tippy toes for a goodbye kiss. When our lips meet, I immediately lose any coherent thought I may have had. I make a point to close my eyes and just *feel*. He runs his fingers through my hair, and I go weak at the knees. When he's done kissing me into a stupor, he starts to back away.

"Does one o'clock sound good for Saturday?" he asks, walking backward to the front door.

I nod.

"Good, I'll see you then."

He turns to open the door and steps outside. When he leans back to grab the handle, his face pulls up into a lazy half-smile. At the rate this is going, I'll be thoroughly fucked in no time...both figuratively and literally. He slowly shuts the door. When I can move my limbs again, I waste no time grabbing my phone off the counter to call Hadley. Time to start round two of my gushing for the day.

EIGHT

c h a s e

I pull up and park in front of my favorite Thai restaurant. I step outside and take a sweeping glance around the parking lot, checking to see if Eric beat me. We're meeting up for lunch in an effort to keep up our ongoing bromance. When I don't see his car anywhere, I whip out my phone and text him: *Here. Where are you?* Then I head on inside and grab a table. An iced tea and four spring rolls later, Eric waltzes in and pulls up a chair.

"What's up?" he greets.

"Dude…you're like thirty minutes late. If this were a real relationship, you'd have blue balls for a week. And you'd owe me roses."

"Oh, please, you're so fucking dramatic. Reel it in."

"Here's a menu. Everything rocks. Nothing sucks. Man, work's kicking my ass today."

"Same here. Is it too early to order a beer?"

I check the time on my phone. "Dude, it's like, noon."

"Yeah, I probably shouldn't," he says reluctantly. "Fucking social norms, they get you every time."

"Tell me about it," I agree.

He grabs a menu and starts skimming. "So, what's good here?"

"Have you already started drinking? Did you not hear what I just said two seconds ago? Everything. I usually go for the Pad Thai."

"Jesus, no need to get snippy," he jokes.

The server comes by to take our order. Once we both rattle off what we want to eat, she collects our menus and walks away.

"So, how'd it go with Mia the other night?" he asks, casually leaning back into his chair.

"It went really well, actually. I took her to Fino, then we drank beer and played mini-golf. Turns out, she's a lot of fun."

"I don't do lame. Not even for friends. You know that. Why are so surprised?"

"I don't know. She seemed pretty uptight at your place, and then again when I picked her up for our date. I wasn't quite sure what I was in store for, but she eventually warmed up. I gotta say, it's a nice change of pace; dating a girl who's cool *and* sexy. All the hot ones are usually crazy."

"No joke. That's my home girl. But I'm telling you right now, if your intentions are shady, stay away from her. She's already been through enough."

Hearing Eric talk about Mia that way strikes a nerve. I know he's looking out for her, but he doesn't need to protect her from me; he should know that.

"My intentions are not shady."

He studies me for a long moment, searching for truth. When he's convinced I'm serious, he nods. "So, what are you up to the rest of the day?"

"Gotta stop by Meg's place after work and check out her flooring. My dad's sending me over there to find out what the issue is. Might be there stuck there all night fixing it. What about you?"

He sits up and leans over the table, resting on his forearms. "Well, I was gonna start drinking until your moral compass put a stop to it. So, not much. More work, followed by the gym, then I'm staying in and chilling for the rest of the night."

"Mia said you're going to ACL this weekend."

"Yeah. You're going, too, right?"

I nod and take a sip of my iced tea.

"Is Mia going?" he asks.

"She's planning on it. At least, that's what she was telling me yesterday."

"Excellent."

"How do you feel about Raven going?"

He frowns and shrugs. "I don't know, man. It is what it is. I've given up on trying with that girl. She can do whatever she wants, and I'll do the same."

Sensing his irritation, I let that one go. Whatever's going on between those two, they can work it out on their own. The last thing I want is to wind up in the middle of all that bullshit.

The server arrives with our food. Smells fucking amazing, and it's nice and hot, too. I pick up my chopsticks and dig in, while Eric spends a good five minutes trying to figure out how to use his. Ultimately, he says, "fuck it," then calls her back over and asks for a fork.

• • •

After calling it a day, I head straight to Megan and Luke's house. I saunter through the front door and into the living room, immediately making myself at home. I grab the remote, turn on the TV, and fall into the couch. Just as I start to get comfortable, my sister emerges from her office. She walks over and hovers with her hands placed firmly on her hips. When I don't look up right away, she loudly clears her throat. *Hate that shit.*

"You know, it wouldn't kill you to return one of my calls once in a while," she says irritably.

"Sorry, sis. Been a little busy lately," I respond while simultaneously channel surfing.

"You're always busy. It doesn't mean you can't give me five minutes of your time."

I swear, the older we get, the more she looks and sounds like my mother. She's tall and slender, she has the same short dark hair framing her face, and her eyes match mine (which we get from our mother). We've been told throughout the years that we look "identical." Personally, I think it's the eye color and tattoos prompting people to draw those comparisons, because other than that, I don't see the resemblance.

She takes a seat next to me and plops her feet onto the coffee table—a wedding gift from Dad and me. We included matching end tables to go with it. Since Meg was fresh out of college when she got married, she didn't have any decent furniture, and neither did Luke. This piece of one of kind. Mahogany with a clear finish. It's masculine but with beveling to soften the edges, and wrought iron knobs on the drawers.

Let's face it; most bachelors don't have the luxury of knowing how to make their own furniture like I do. Even if they did, I doubt they'd put in the time. Most men I know couldn't care less about side tables.

"What's new?" Meg asks.

"Work. Oh, and I broke things off with Christa," I say nonchalantly.

"Really?!" She can't hide the satisfaction in her voice. Meg never cared too much for Christa. This was another reason why I never pursued anything more. If you can't get along with my parents or my sister, it's probably not going to work out. "What made you decide to do that?"

"I wasn't feeling it anymore...and I met someone else," I cave.

That gets her attention. She shifts her body toward mine. I look back and forth between her and the TV.

"Nosey much?" I ask.

"I'm your sister; I'm allowed to be nosey. If a new girl's come into the picture, I wanna know about it."

"It's not that big of a deal. We're casually dating."

"It can't be that casual if you dropped Christa for her," she pushes.

She's right, but she doesn't need to know that. I'm also trying not to get my hopes up, just in case things don't work out with Mia.

"Meg, stop trying to make a big deal out of it."

"What's her name?"

"Mia."

"Where did you meet her?"

"At one of Eric's parties. She's a friend of Raven's."

"What does she do for a living?"

"She doesn't have a job yet. She just moved down here a week ago."

"How old is she?"

"Jesus, I don't know, my age, a couple years younger. Can we lay off with the third degree?"

"Fine. Don't get your panties in a twist. I was just asking," she says defensively.

"I get that, but it's none of your business."

"Jeez, what crawled up your ass and died today?"

Just as the words leave her mouth, you can practically see the glow of the lightbulb going off in her head. "Wait a second, you're keeping this a secret because you like her, don't you?"

"Meg, let it go," I warn.

"I'm right, aren't I? You care about this girl. That's why you're being so evasive."

"I'm not being evasive and she's not a dirty little secret. I was completely forthcoming until you decided to turn it into a fucking interrogation."

I stand up and stride into the kitchen to grab a bottle of water out of the fridge, which is my way of letting her know that I'm done with this conversation. Meg continues to watch me intently from the couch. I twist the cap off and down a quarter of the bottle. The water feels cold and refreshing as it makes its way down my throat, washing away the sawdust taste I've had from working all day.

Suddenly, I hear the garage door open. I look back to Meg and she gives me a tight, apologetic smile.

"Yes, I like her," I admit.

Before she has a chance to respond, the door to the house swings open and Luke walks in. He's dressed in one of his many expensive suits. He sets his keys and wallet down on the counter, walks over, and kisses my sister on the cheek.

"Hey, baby," he greets.

"Hey, how was work?"

"Good. Closed the Southeast Cineplex deal," he says proudly, loosening his tie. Luke's in advertising.

"That's great, babe! Hey, don't forget about dinner with my parents tonight," she reminds him.

Luke nods and walks over to where I'm standing. He reaches out and pulls me in for a one-arm hug.

"Hey, Chase, how's it going?"

"It's going well," I reply. "Just came here to check out the floor. I'd rather address more important things, though—like when are you going to come party with my buddies and me again?"

"Uh, never, jackass," my sister intervenes. "Quit trying to steal my husband."

Last time Luke came out with the boys and me, we ended up getting him completely trashed and then dragged him to a strip club downtown. Megan was furious. She gave me hell for weeks afterward and made me promise to never do it again. I gave her my word and, unfortunately, Luke has been on his best behavior ever since.

I'm not sure why, but I always seem to be in hot water over something. It's kind of been the main theme throughout my entire life.

"I was in the doghouse for days last time," he confesses.

"You and me both, buddy," I smirk.

Megan glares at me.

See? Hot water.

"All right, enough. Chase, you came over to check out the floor, so let me show you where it's messed up. Then we can head to Mom and Dad's."

"Sounds good."

• • •

By the time I make it back home, it's well past ten. Feeling beat from all the running around I did today, I skip my nightly workout routine and head straight to my room so I can change into sweats. I plug my phone in so it can charge overnight, and as I'm looking down at the screen, I get a sudden, overwhelming urge to text Mia.

Me: *How was your day?*

A minute or so goes by before I receive a response.

Mia: *It was good. How was yours?*

Me: *Busy, but good. What are you up to?*

In order to keep myself distracted between messages, I start sifting through all of the emails that I rarely ever check. When my phone vibrates, I quickly switch back over.

Mia: *In bed reading a book. You?*

Me: *Thinking about you :)*

Mia: *Cheesy.*

I can picture her rolling her eyes while she typed that one out and it makes me smile.

Me: *You like it, don't deny it. What are you reading?*

Mia: *Hardly…*

Me: *Hardly doesn't qualify as not at all. And you still haven't told me what you're reading. *Gasp* Are you reading smut? Don't you dare lie to me.*

Mia: *You wish. Go to bed.*

Me: *Are you?*

Mia: *GO TO BED!*

Me: *I knew it! You totally are. I approve and applaud.*

Mia: *Omg, don't you ever stop?*

Me: *Nope. I can go All. Night. Long.*

Mia: *Um…*

Seeing an opportunity, I strike.

Me: *Can I call you?*

Mia: *I suppose.*

I press the call button and she picks up almost immediately. We spend the next hour talking to each other about anything and everything. I can't remember the last time I spent this much time talking to anyone on the phone—let alone a woman I'm interested in. It's only when I hear her steady breathing on the other end of the line that I finally decide to hang up for the night.

NINE

a　m　e　l　i　a

Zilker Park is packed. Most of the people here are either drinking, or they're already drunk—I'm the former...for now. This is an all-day event, so pacing myself is the key to a fabulous experience. I decided to ride with Eric so that way Chase didn't have to go out of his way pick me up. He told me it wasn't a big deal, that he'd be happy to come get me, but I'd insisted. Besides, I haven't seen Eric since the night of the party.

We raided the food carts beforehand. I won't even tell you how many wings I ate. It's straight-up repulsive, and I'm not in the mood to be judged. But I did it for the greater good, I promise. I'm no fun to be around when I'm hungry. It's the equivalent to being "on the rag" and finding out that my chocolate stash has been depleted. Someone will surely die.

Since some of the streets are closed off (and parking within a five-mile radius is impossible), Eric had to park way out in the middle of bumfuck nowhere. I'm not complaining, though. It gave me a chance to walk those wings off, which consequently gave me a craving for more beer.

"You thirsty?" Eric asks, reading my mind.

"God, yes."

"Me too. How about I buy and you fly?"

"Deal."

He reaches into his back pocket to grab his wallet, pulls out a crisp twenty, folds it between his fingers, and holds it out in front of me. I snag the bill and look around for the closest place to get drinks. There's a beer tent on my radar, but a zillion people are standing in the way. It looks like I'm going to be doing some more walking. *Whatever. I've got nothing but time on my hands.*

I patiently wait in line. Grabbing our beers, I walk back through the enormous crowd and attempt to find Eric. So far, I've managed to keep most of the beer contained, but some spilled onto my clothes when other people collided with me. Good thing I dressed appropriately. I'm sporting jeans and a low-cut T-shirt. Members of The Clash are splashed across the front with tour dates listed on the back. My hair is done in a loose fishtail braid that hooks around to the side, and my eyes are hidden beneath my sunglasses—naturally.

"Hey, Bono, over here!" Eric yells. I spot his hand in the air, motioning me to come his way. He's found a great place for us to stand. It's a ways out from the stage, but it's still a good view.

"Thanks, Strawberry," he says once I reach him. I place his change in one hand and his drink in the other. I think it's safe to assume that at this rate, we won't be driving home.

"Thanks for paying."

"Of course," he winks.

We stand and sip our beers, enjoying the moment while waiting for Broken Bells to perform. It's hot out today, but between the alcohol and the masses of awesome people surrounding us, we're going to be just fine.

"So..." Eric looks down. "What's the deal with you and Chase?"

I shrug and take another long sip of beer. Based on his awkward demeanor, I'm guessing Eric feels conflicted about two of his closest friends casually dating. Can't say I blame him. It's a situation that has the potential to end badly.

"I don't know. We went out Monday night and then he stopped by the apartment on Tuesday. That's the last time I saw him."

"But you've heard from him, right?"

I nod. "We've been texting each other all week."

"Good," he says. He seems pleased, which makes me pleased.

A few minutes go by before I work up the courage to ask a question that I'm not entirely sure I want to know the answer to.

"Hey, Eric?" I tilt my head up.

He looks down at me and smiles. "Yeah?"

"What's the deal with Chase and Christa?"

He lifts an eyebrow. "Isn't that something you should ask Chase about?"

He's right. I shouldn't be asking him, but it's been in the back of my mind since the night I met Chase. I didn't want to bring it up so soon. I really like him and I don't want to give him a reason to run off or think that I'm jealous. I'm sure if he hadn't met me, he probably would've gone home with her at the party that first night. It's like a scab I can't stop picking at. Morbid curiosity is a bitch.

"You're right. I'm sorry I'm asking you. He's given me no reason to doubt him thus far, but I trust you, Eric. If they're still hooking up, I don't want to get in the middle and wind up getting screwed over."

He sighs. "You do realize I'm breaking guy code, right?"

"Please," I beg.

He looks around the crowd uncomfortably, like he's being put on the spot.

"As far as I know that's over between them—for now." He runs a hand through his blond hair. "Listen, you have to understand that Chase is a lot like me. It's why we get along so well. We've been each other's wingman for years. It's our thing. We don't like to lock ourselves down and commit to one girl."

My stomach drops.

"That being said, I firmly believe that if he told you it's over between them, then it's over. We may be womanizers, but we aren't liars. And I don't think he'd juggle you and Christa at the same time."

"What do you mean it's over between them 'for now'?"

"Christa is Chase's constant. They've never been exclusive, but she was never just a random booty call. She has some kind of hold over him. She's the only girl that's gotten under his skin since Nicole."

"Who's Nicole?" I ask.

Eric winces, shaking his head. "You aren't going to hear about that one from me. I've already said more than I should."

I chug the rest of my beer. I've been looking forward to ACL all week, but now my mood has soured. Serves me right for asking a question I didn't want to know the answer to in the first place. Eric gives me a sympathetic look. I hate it when people look at me that way. I don't want or need his pity.

"You're reading too much into this, Mia. Don't overanalyze it. He likes you. He wouldn't be wasting his time taking you out on dates and showing up at your apartment just to see you if he didn't. Trust me."

I smack my lips together and stare straight ahead. Physically, I'm here, but my head is off somewhere else. I need another drink...or three.

"I'm going to find the bathrooms and grab another beer. Want one?"

"Nah, I'm still good on this one," he says, raising his can.

Feeling my phone vibrate, I reach into my pocket and pull it out. I have two messages—one from Chase, one from Raven.

Chase: *Parking and walking that way. I'll call you when I get close. Can't wait to see you :)*

Seeing his message softens me a little. I close my eyes and take a few deep breaths to clear my head. The alcohol is intensifying my emotions. Why do I even care? It makes me feel better to know that Eric believes he really likes me, but I can't stop thinking about him and Christa. Knowing that she gets to him, gets to me. I quickly pull up Raven's message to help distract me.

Raven: *Just got off work. Heading home to change and then I'll drive straight there. Also, if I know Eric, he'll be probably be wasted by the time I arrive, so I can drive us back.*

I type out a response and head off in search for a bathroom. I need to slow down on the beer now that I'll be breaking the seal, because once the show starts, I don't want to have to make thirty trips to pee. *Oh, and note to self: hydrate.*

When I meet up with Eric again, I'm much more relaxed and carefree. Funny how when you're buzzed, time seems to slow down and speed up at the same time. It's like everything blurs together and your mind is trying to make sense of it all. I can't even tell you the last time I felt this much like my own age.

Just then, a hard body comes up behind me and I instantly know who it is without looking. My heart leaps as two large hands settle on my hips. Soft lips gently press against the side of my neck. I tilt my head back to give him better access. My eyes flutter closed and my entire body responds to that one simple gesture. I blame the alcohol. He continues to trail kisses up my throat, his rough hands tightening on my hips. The stubble on his face tickles my skin and drives me wild.

To my disappointment, he stops and pulls back to press his nose to my hair, inhaling deeply. I secretly give myself three big cheers for deciding to wash it this morning. He presses a chaste kiss to my head and lowers his lips to my ear. "Mmm, you smell good," he murmurs, appreciative.

I groan. Jeez, I can't concentrate when he says things like that. He's distracting enough to look at. I don't need him giving me compliments.

"Jesus, you two—get a room," Eric teases.

Chase chuckles against my ear and nips the lobe in good humor as I'm rudely brought back to reality. I'd gotten so caught up in what he was doing, that I forgot Eric was standing right next to us. My body instantly cools at his interruption and my cheeks burn with embarrassment. Thankfully, everyone's attention is summoned to the stage for Broken Bells. I recognize the first few notes of "October," and the crowd erupts in cheers.

When the show ends, I check my phone. Raven's called twice already. There's no way I'll be able to hear with all the commotion, so I let Chase and Eric know I'll be back shortly.

When I get far enough away, I call her back. She answers on the second ring.

"Hey, Mia!"

"Hey, how close are you?"

"Um, it looks like I'm a couple blocks away. I'm walking that way right now."

"Okay, I'll keep an eye out for you."

"Are Eric and Chase with you?"

"Yes and no."

I explain that the guys are here, but they stayed behind. I look around and give her some descriptions, hoping she'll have some idea of where to find me. Five minutes later, I see her making her way toward me. She looks fierce and confident as she struts over the grass like it's a damn runway. Only Raven would find it practical to wear heels to an event like this.

"I need a drink," she professes.

"Rough night at the restaurant?"

"*Very,*" she stresses.

"Should we make it a double?"

"No. I'm driving tonight," she reminds me.

"Oh, right. Good call."

Raven's rule is one drink only on the nights she's driving. Because she's a pretty cautious person by nature, she doesn't usually push it. As someone who lost their dad to a drunk driver, I appreciate that.

"Let's stop by the bathrooms on the way."

"Broke the seal, did you?" she asks, her eyes glittering with humor.

I nod and she laughs.

I'm cutting myself off. After five, I start getting sloppy and obnoxious. Nobody likes a hot mess. That's the last impression I want to make on Chase, or anyone else for that matter. I grab Raven's hand and we begin our hunt for Eric and Chase. They're much harder to find this time. I try to weave us around the crowd to avoid colliding with other people. Raven's yelling something but I can't hear her over the music. Once we reach a less crowded spot, we stop and scan.

"I don't see them anywhere!" I yell in her ear.

"Me neither!" she yells back.

It doesn't help that I'm short and can't see over anyone in front of me. Suddenly, Raven tugs on my arm. I look back and she points off to the side. Chase and Eric are both standing a few feet away from us with two girls hanging around them.

My fists clench up, and I immediately go into defensive, ass-kicking mode. The girl with Chase has long black hair and beautiful dark skin. She's dressed in a pair of cowgirl boots, an obscenely short skirt, and a blue halter top that doesn't quite cover her mid-drift. She's gorgeous and I immediately hate her for that. I watch her boldly reach out and brush her fingers along Chase's upper arm, smiling sweetly at him. She's flirting—heavily. He isn't touching her in return, but he's not stopping her either.

My blood boils.

"What the fuck is she doing?" Raven yells.

I turn back around to see her seething. Knowing that she's pissed in my honor makes me love her all the more. I really do have the best friends.

"Seriously, why is he even entertaining the thought of her? He's supposed to be with me. Clueless idiot!" she shouts.

Damn straight.

Wait….

What?

I follow her line of vision. Then it hits me. Raven's not angry on my behalf, she's jealous of this woman flirting with Eric.

Raven has feelings for Eric?

The thought is blowing my mind. *How did I not see this coming? Has something gone down between the two of them that I don't know about?* I've been so wrapped up in Chase lately that I missed something that was so close in front of me, it could reach out and bitch-slap me across the face.

I cross my arms over my chest. "Rave, tell me what's going on."

She tears her gaze away from Eric and I catch a glimpse of hurt in her eyes. She straightens up and composes herself, concealing her emotions.

"Later," she mouths.

I drop my arms and let that pacify me for now, but come later tonight, I was getting some answers. Raven flips her hair behind her shoulder and tugs down on the hem of her cami. She isn't going to drool over Eric, and she isn't going to take shit from these girls.

She turns to me and does the same thing with my shirt to show a little more cleavage. Luckily, I'm wearing my best bra tonight, which makes my boobs look fantastic. She removes the hair tie from the end of my braid and runs her fingers through my long tresses. The sensations ripple all across my scalp and down my spine. Head rubs are my weakness, and with the loose way I'm feeling, I may end up shacking up with her instead of Chase by the time the night is over.

"Come on. Whatever you do, don't let them see you sweat. That's giving them a satisfaction they don't deserve." She grabs my hand and leads the way.

I internally put up my steel resolve as we make our way over there. When we approach them from behind, I see Chase's back tighten up as if he senses my presence. The alcohol is making my mind wander. I'm imagining what his bare back looks like and how it would feel to run my fingernails down it. Then I remind myself to keep my eye on the prize—which isn't Chase.

The guys turn around to face us and Chase's anxious gaze finds mine. He's on edge, watching me intently. He's gauging my reaction to see if I'm pissed. I give absolutely nothing away. Instead, I let the music distract me and focus on dancing to deflect those pesky emotions. If I repeatedly tell myself I don't care, then it's bound to come true. Self-deluding is my thing.

His eyes move down to my chest and his expression softens, filling with heat and desire.

Yeah, go right ahead and salivate.

I turn to check on Raven's questionable state of mind. On the surface, she looks like her usual, cheerful self, but I know better. She gives me a certain look out of the corner of her eye, one that tells me she has an ace up her sleeve.

"Are y'all going to introduce us to your friends, or are we just supposed to pull their names out of thin air?" Subtlety and patience are not her strong points today.

Instantly remembering that they have company behind them, the guys refocus their attention. I use their temporary distraction to look at Raven like she's batshit crazy. She brushes it off and stares back at me with a stoic expression.

"Mia, Raven, this is Tamika. Tamika works with me at Surge. This is her friend Sasha. I was just telling her how surprised I was to see her here. I figured she was working the bar tonight, but she happened to get the night off," Chase explains, more so to me than to Raven.

How convenient.

Raven steps between Eric and Chase to shake both of the girls' hands and introduces herself. I quickly step forward to do the same.

"So, how do you know Eric?" Raven asks Sasha curiously.

"I met him at Chase's place, actually. Tamika invited me over one night and we all hung out together."

It's a good thing I'm standing in front of Chase now because I can't hide the jealousy I feel when I hear her say that. I know he has a history, but running into his "history" everywhere is quickly wearing thin.

"Is that so?" Raven asks coyly. "Well, Mia and I were thinking about doing some bar hopping tonight to pick up some guys. Y'all should join. It'll be more fun as a group. What do you say, ladies?"

The fuck? Has she officially lost her mind?

"Um, sure. Sounds like fun, I guess," Tamika says, hesitant.

"Excellent!" Raven exclaims.

I look over my shoulder to assess the guys' reactions. Eric looks confused, and Chase looks pissed off. I feel a twinge of guilt but push it aside and continue with the facade we have going on. If I break now, Raven will kill me. But if I go through with her plan, Chase will be furious. There's no winning for me in this scenario. Since I don't know what Chase's intentions are with Tamika, I stick with Raven on this one. Chicks before dicks.

Once all the bands finish, we walk downtown to the local bars. If it were under different circumstances, I might actually like Tamika and Sasha. They're pretty fun to party with, and despite the bizarre situation we're in, I must admit, I'm having a good time.

Chase and Eric have had their hands full cock-blocking all of the other guys that keep hitting on us. Eric is only growing more and more irritated as the night goes on, but none of us care—least of all, Raven. Chase, on the other hand, is trickier. I know he's jealous, but he's masking it well.

We're all walking down the street to our next bar when Raven sees the sign for Surge. There's a decent-sized line and she quickly pulls me aside to stand in it. While we're waiting for the line to move forward, us girls talk about how awesome the shows were tonight. In the middle of our discussion, I look over to find Chase staring straight at me, his gaze intense and unwavering. It's like he's trying to tell me something. He makes no effort to join in on the conversation, but he doesn't look away, either.

Once everyone but Chase and Tamika show their ID's to the doormen, we're in. Raven wasn't kidding when she said this place was a hot spot. The club is packed wall-to-wall. We walk down a couple steps onto the main floor, which is highlighted with blue lights. There's a large wraparound bar in front of us and a dance floor off to the left. There's a DJ booth set up and on either side there are cages—fully complete with women dancing seductively inside. The lighting is pretty dim, giving the club a more erotic feel. The bartenders are slammed, frantically running back and forth between impatient customers and the cash register.

Against my will, Raven abruptly grabs my hand and makes a beeline for the dance floor. Tamika runs up to the bar to say hi to her co-workers. Sasha grabs Eric to dance and Chase disappears somewhere into the crowd.

Watching Eric dance with Sasha only spurs Raven. It's starting to become a petty contest of who can rile up who more. When Raven grabs the occasional guy, Eric kicks up the dirty dancing a notch with Sasha. Seeing the two of them rub up against each other has to be killing Raven, but she's showing absolutely no sign of being upset.

I continue what feels like a Dance Marathon until my body can't take it anymore. There's no way Raven's going to let me leave. She's on a mission, and apparently, she likes Eric more than either of us realized, because she seems hell-bent on proving her point.

When the music starts to slow, I decide that it's a good time for a break. I walk over to Raven and tell her that I need to hit the bathroom and take a breather, much to her dismay.

I squeeze my way off the dance floor to find the restrooms. Locating them at the back of the club, I waste no time getting there. I turn down a long hallway and see the sign that says "Women" but before I can walk in there, I feel a hard body come up behind me and force me into a room that's supposed to be for employees only.

Swiftly turning around, I see Chase shut and lock the door, his gaze trapping mine. His face is hard, cold, and angry but his eyes are burning with desire. He slowly saunters toward me. I stand completely still and try to hold onto my indifference. I'm losing that battle at a rapid rate. He presses a palm flat against my stomach and my body shudders with sheer delight. He walks me backward until I have nowhere else to go. The wall cuts me off.

Placing his hands on either side of my head, he cages me in. My heart is pounding and my chest is rising and falling, drawing Chase's attention to it. Bringing his eyes back to mine, he carefully leans forward towards my cleavage and lets out a slow, cool breath. It immediately hits my damp chest and I feel my sex clench in response. I lay my head back against the wall and look up to the ceiling, arching my back, silently begging him not to stop.

He doesn't.

My nipples tighten and the hair on my arms rises. He makes no move to touch me, he simply continues to blow cool spouts of air all over my heated body. My chest, my neck, and my face. He smells like some spice that I can't quite pinpoint, and his own, personal scent.

"Are you done playing around?" he whispers harshly in my ear.

"I'm not playing around," I lie.

He brings his knee up between my legs and strokes me against my jeans with a firm, but gentle pressure. The friction is delicious and all I can focus on is my body's sensations shooting off everywhere.

"Are you sure about that?" He's breathing just as hard as I am.

I moan as he strokes me again. My hands form fists at my sides. I try to control my body's reaction but it's no use. Chase is everywhere. He's on my body, he's in my head, and he's slowly wedging his way into my heart.

"Does that feel good, Amelia?"

I close my eyes and say nothing. I feel his hair lightly brush against my skin as he lays a kiss down on the top swell of each of my breasts, and then his lips are back at my ear.

"Do you like it when I do that?" he rasps.

I whimper. *Holy fuck, I'm going to explode.* My knees start to buckle and I sink down onto his thigh. My hips start a slow gyration against his leg, the seam of my jeans rubbing perfectly against the right spot. I stick my palms flat against the wall and use that as support to continue my grind on him. I lock onto his gaze and pour every ounce of desire I'm feeling into him. My body is wound so tight. He looks like he's about to combust just watching me do this to myself. I don't care about being shy. It feels too good.

Suddenly, he reaches down to grab my ass. He hoists me up and I wrap my legs around his torso. He halts my movements and I can feel how rock hard he is through his jeans. He laces his fingers through mine and lifts both our hands up and rests them on the wall above my head. His deep blue eyes are burning into mine. I'm sexually frustrated and I want the friction back.

"Does it drive you crazy when I do that?"

I swallow hard and nod.

"Good, because you've been driving me crazy all fucking night. Do you have any idea how pissed I am that you tried to pick up guys? Am I a toy to you? Something you think you can play with?"

"Am I just a toy for *you* to play with?" I snap, sending his question right back. My sexual frustration is now turning into anger. I don't know which I want to do more—slap the shit out of him, or screw his brains out.

Confusion washes over his face.

"What are you talking about? Why would you say that? I think I've been pretty upfront with how I feel about you," he defends.

Is he joking right now? What an idiot.

I narrow my gaze and try to break his hold on my body, but he doesn't budge. It's clear he isn't going to let me go until we hash this out.

"Oh, really? Then explain Christa and Tamika to me. What are they to you? What am I to you, huh? One of many? A casual fucking fling? Because if that's where this is headed, we really need to stop."

That was it. I just gave him his easy out.

He releases a hand and gently caresses my face. I'm trying to keep my guard up but the way he's looking at me is making that task impossible.

"You are not a casual fling. Okay? You are the only girl that I'm seeing, and I fully intend to keep it that way. Tamika works with me, and we've hung out together before, but we've never slept together. Not once. I don't dip my pen in company ink, so to speak. And as far as Christa goes, I told you that's over between us."

"For how long? A week? And why were you letting Tamika put the moves on you?" I accuse.

He grabs ahold of my hips and lifts me off, setting me down on my feet. He steps back and runs his hands through his hair. He seems to do that a lot when he's nervous or irritated. I may not know him that well yet, but I have picked up on that tic. Eric has the same habit.

"Tamika is naturally a flirty person. You learn to get used to it and not think much of it, but I swear I'm not interested in her that way. I'm interested in you. I wasn't hitting on her despite what it may have looked like.

"As for Christa, yes, she and I have a history, but the difference now is I have feelings for someone else. That's never happened before when she and I were sleeping around. I wouldn't jeopardize what you and I potentially have here. I care about you, Mia," he confesses.

Relief washes over me and I begin to thaw a little. I knew he wasn't hitting on Tamika tonight. Despite my jealousy, I only saw her flirting with him, he never reciprocated. Deep down, I also believe him when he says he and Christa are done messing around. As of right now, I have no real reason not to trust Chase. Sure, he has a past, but he hasn't done anything to hurt me.

"I'm sorry I went along with Raven's plan. That wasn't very considerate of me. To be honest, I wasn't actively seeking out guys. When I left to go meet up with Raven and bring her back to our spot, she saw Sasha flirting with Eric and lost it. Tonight wasn't about getting back at you; it was Raven's way of trying to get to Eric," I explain.

He looks relieved. "Why didn't you say something? I was starting to think my feelings for you were one-sided."

"I should have, but she was on a rampage and I kinda got sucked in. One minute we were all having a good time and I was thinking I'd get some alone time with you, and then the next minute, we saw them flirting with you guys and it all went downhill from there."

Sighing, Chase pulls me into his arms and lays my head against his chest. I close my eyes and listen to the sound of his heart beating while he holds me. Every so often, he kisses my head and runs his hands up and down my back.

"Those two really need to figure their situation out," he says.

"You're telling me. I didn't even know there was a situation until tonight."

"Eric has been infatuated with her for years, but she never seemed to be interested in him that way. Apparently, now she is." He chuckles.

Tonight is the first night where I felt comfortable enough to have a raw conversation with him. Feels like something's changed between us. I just hope he notices it too.

"We should get back. I can't believe someone hasn't come looking for us," he smirks.

"Yeah," I reluctantly agree. "I need to go check on Raven and see how she's doing." I grab onto the door handle but Chase reaches out and pulls me back.

"By the way, you look amazing tonight. I know I didn't get a chance to tell you that earlier, so I wanted to tell you now."

I smile. "Awe, thank you."

"Awe, you're welcome," he teases. "What do you say we get out of here and have that alone time you mentioned?"

"Whatever," I say indifferently. "I was thinking maybe we could bring one of those guys back with us that hit on me earlier. What do you say?"

He narrows his eyes and scowls. "Not. Funny."

"Maybe I should make you jealous more often. It's a sexy look on you."

"Behave," he warns.

"Never," I promise.

He responds to that by giving me a good smack on the ass.

And they say romance is dead.

TEN

c h a s e

"My place or yours?" I ask Mia.

"Definitely mine. I want to be there for Raven just in case she needs a friend to talk to about Eric."

I can live with that. I really wanted her to choose my place because I don't live with any roommates, but I understand her reasoning.

We walk back out front and search around for everyone who came with us. Thanks to Raven, that's a longer list of people than necessary. I about lost my shit when she invited Tamika and Sasha to pick up guys with her and Mia. I knew she was just toying with Eric, which pissed me off even more when she pulled Mia into it. There's no way in hell I was going to let another guy get within ten feet of her. I know she isn't technically my girl yet, but I'll be damned if I let some other guy walk out of here with her. If I'm going down, I'm going down for a good reason. Not some false assumption that I'm into someone else.

Spotting Tamika over at the bar, I place my hand on the middle of Mia's back and steer her over there so we can say goodbye.

"Oh, hey! I was wondering where everyone went," Tamika says once we reach her.

"Yeah, sorry. I think Eric, Raven, and Sasha are still dancing. I had to go to the bathroom to cool down for a minute," Mia explains.

She looks up to give me an indulgent smile and bites down on her bottom lip like the little tease she is. Cool down, my ass. I was so wound up from watching her rub up against me, I almost came undone. I've had my fair share of women, but the way Mia makes me feel, there's no comparison. She's a force of nature that I can't control and never saw coming. She barreled into my life with no warning whatsoever and annihilated everything I thought I knew about what I wanted from a woman—from a relationship.

"I see. So where we headed next?" Tamika asks eagerly.

"Actually, we're going to call it a night."

"Oh, okay," she says, disappointed. "Well, thanks for inviting us to come out. I had a great time, and I'm sure Sasha did, too."

"You okay to drive?" I check.

"Yeah, I haven't had that much."

Mia looks up at me adoringly like she's seeing me in a different light for the first time. I shoot her a confused look as she tries to fight the cute smile that's forming on her face. She needs to stop looking at me like that if she wants me to behave myself, but we'll talk about that later.

"Alright, look out for yourself tonight and I'll see you tomorrow at work."

"See you then, Chase," she replies.

I grab Mia's hand and push through all of the people. I see Eric and Sasha grinding on each other, but Raven is nowhere to be found. I turn back around to Mia.

"Why don't you try to find Raven and I'll meet you outside after I let Eric and Sasha know what's going on," I suggest.

She nods and walks off.

I walk up to Eric and Sasha, who are so glued to one another, they don't seem to notice anything or anyone else around them. I grab Eric's upper arm and peel him away for a minute.

"What the hell, Chase? Can't you see I'm busy?" he asks in an annoyed tone.

"I know. I'm just letting you know that Mia and I are headed back to her place, and possibly Raven, too, if we can find her."

"Alright I'll catch up with all y'all later," he says. He turns to grab Sasha again, but I pull him back to me once more.

"Hey, for what it's worth, she's into you," I tell him.

"No shit she's into me. Now if you let go of my arm, I can get back to her and possibly get laid later."

I shake my head.

"Not Sasha, dude. Raven. Raven is into you."

"What?"

"I'm serious. That's why she's been on such a warpath tonight. Seeing you with Sasha set her off."

Eric gives me a mixed look of pure disbelief and annoyance. He shakes his head in frustration while he processes what I've just said. Since I've been there and done that, I decide to give him some unsolicited, but much needed, advice.

"Eric, you've liked that girl forever, man. If there's even the slightest chance that she wants you, isn't that worth looking into?"

He shakes his head. "It's not that simple. I don't know what she wants from me anymore. The only time she's interested, is when the threat of another girl is in the picture. It's the classic case of she wants what she can't have. I'm not going to be strung along like some fucking puppet. It's not my job to be at her beck and call."

"I think it's more than that," I say, in Raven's defense.

"It doesn't matter. She needs to figure her shit out. Her inability to make up her mind is not my problem," he says adamantly.

I drop the subject and let him know that I'll be driving Mia home. Since he intends to bring Sasha back to his place tonight, he's more than happy with that arrangement.

I leave them to it and head for the exit to wait out front for Mia. When I step outside, I see that there is still a long line of people waiting to get in. There's a breeze tonight and it instantly cools me down. All of the buildings are lit up downtown, which makes the city look awesome. The streets and sidewalks are filled with people— mainly college students—who are all out having a good time.

A minute or two goes by and just as I'm starting to get impatient, Mia and Raven come walking out hand-in-hand. Raven's face is flushed and I'm not sure if it's from all of the dancing she was doing or whether she's been crying. Mia releases her hand, strolls over to me, and rests her hands on my shoulders.

"Raven is going to drive herself back to the apartment. Is it okay if I ride with her instead and meet you there?" she asks, eyes hopeful.

I reach out and tuck a strand of hair behind her ear and caress her cheek. "Of course. I'll meet you there."

"Thank you," she mouths in appreciation.

I give her a slight nod and lean in to kiss her cheek. I fish my keys out of my pocket and start the long walk to get back to my car. I already know these next fifteen minutes are going to painfully creep by.

I pull into their apartment complex and immediately spot Raven's car. Good. I drove slow on purpose, hoping they would beat me back here so I didn't have to sit and wait. When I reach their door, I give it a couple of hard knocks. The door opens up and Raven steps aside to let me in.

"Mia's in the shower. She'll be out shortly. You can either hang out here or head into her room and wait for her in there. Either way, don't be a pervert about it," she says, stepping out. She closes the door behind her, leaving me alone with my thoughts of Mia showering right down the hall.

Now, if I were being a gentleman, I'd wait out in the living room. But when all I can think about is a stream of water running down her wet, naked body, and her hands running up and down certain areas to rub soap on herself...well...shit can you really blame me for choosing to wait in the bedroom? I figure if she doesn't want me in there, then she can kick me out herself.

I head down the hall and stop in between the two bedrooms. *Which one is hers?* I open the door on the left and see that everything is neat and organized. Definitely *not* Mia's room. I close the door and open the bedroom door on the right. There's a full bed and a nightstand, but those are the only pieces of furniture she has in here. Some of her clothes are strewn out over her bed and on the floor, including the outfit she was wearing tonight. She doesn't have much stuff. It looks like she's living out of a suitcase.

What happened to her? I have a feeling it's been a while since Mia truly felt welcome anywhere. I'm going to give her that feeling back. I want her to feel safe, settled, and comfortable.

I walk up to the bed and crawl across it. Once I reach the head of the mattress, I lay down on my side so that I'm facing the door for when she walks in. I pull out my phone and browse Instagram while I anxiously wait for her finish showering.

Hearing the bathroom door open, I toss my phone to the side. Mia walks in wearing a tight, pale-purple tank, and large charcoal sweatpants. Her hair is down, messy, and soaking wet. *Fuck me, she's gorgeous, even in sweats.* She freezes when she sees me, her face unreadable.

"What are you doing in here?" she asks.

"Raven told me I could wait out there or in here. Which one did you honestly think I was gonna go with?"

I prop my elbow on the bed and rest my head as I continue to drink her in. She just stands there, eying me heatedly. I take the opportunity to play with her.

"See something you like?" I tease.

"Yeah, actually, I do. I see something I *really* like," she stresses.

"What a coincidence. I also happen to see something I really like," I say, eyeing her up and down.

She walks to the side of the bed, places both her hands on the mattress, and leans into me. She smells divine. Like strawberries and vanilla. I instantly want a taste but refrain from touching her. She brings her mouth to my ear and whispers, "I'll give you a hint, what I see brings me comfort and heats me up in all the right ways, and I'd probably get a little jealous if I saw it on anyone else, because it's *mine*." She licks the outer shell of my ear and I about lose it.

I feel her pulling at something underneath my leg. I lift my body to help her out, and she grabs a black Pink Floyd hoodie and slips it on. "Mmmm, now that's what I'm talking about," she says, smelling the inside of the hoodie and exhaling in contentment.

What a tease.

I make a tsking sound as I bring both of my legs around the side of the bed and stand up in front of her. I grab her by the waist and launch her onto the bed.

"Ahh!" She hits the bed with a light thud and giggles. Lifting herself up, she scoots back against the headboard.

I close the bedroom door and walk around to the end of the bed, placing my knee down. The mattress dips with my weight as I slowly crawl towards her. I grab her ankle, and pull her my way, until she's lying flat beneath me. Her top rides up a little bit, and I can see a small patch of skin where her shirt ends and the sweatpants begin. I lean forward and grab her hips to bring the spot of skin to my lips. She gasps as I lay the first kiss down. I continue to rain kisses all over her torso, over her shirt, and up her neck as if I'm worshipping her.

My fingers travel along the inside of her arms until I reach her palms and intertwine our fingers. I hover over her and pin her weight with my hips. Her gorgeous eyes are searing with desire and her breathing has picked up. I gently bite down on the top swell of her breast and suck. Mia moans and tries to buck her hips against me. She whines in protest when I block her. I'm guessing it's been a while. I'm going to take my sweet time and torture her before I give her what she wants.

"Chase?" she breathes.

"Yeah, baby?"

"Touch me," she begs.

"Where?"

"Everywhere," she says, her eyes filled with wonder.

I begin to trace my fingers down her body, over her clothes. She shakes her head back and forth, vigorously. I instantly stop and look up, feeling her out.

"No, Chase. Under my clothes," she says softly. Her cheeks turn pink and I know she's embarrassed. We need to work on that right now. I'm going to make sure she's never embarrassed to ask me for what she wants. If she needs something, I'm going to be the one to give it to her. I fist my hand in her wet hair and firmly hold her in place until she's gazing up into my eyes. I need her to be in a better headspace before I can continue this.

"Mia, don't ever be afraid or ashamed to tell me what you want, okay?"

She doesn't say anything.

"Okay?" I gently nudge.

She lets out a nervous breath and nods. I'm going to make it my mission to fire her up so she's no longer focusing on her nerves. I want her completely confident with me.

"Tell me what you want," I command. My grip on her hair tightens and I bring my hand to cup and tease her through her sweatpants. She lets out a high-pitched, needy sound.

"Say it," I demand.

"You," she gasps. "I...I want you. God, please don't stop," she begs.

"Tell me exactly what you want me to do to you. Be filthy and explicit."

"I want you to take my clothes off and fuck me with your mouth."

"Fuck what with my mouth?" I ask, my eyes burning with heat. I want to hear her say it.

Silence.

"Say it, Mia," I challenge. I roll my hips into her and her eyes roll back in bliss.

"No," she breathes.

Stubborn woman.

I slowly peel her pants off her to reveal a gorgeous set of tanned legs. She probably thinks she's getting what she wants without asking for it, but she's wrong.

She lifts her hips, silently begging me for it.

I place my mouth against her pussy and let out a heated breath, making her groan. She's soaking wet. I can feel it right through her panties. She needs to say it soon because I don't know how much longer I can hold out before I taste her. "Say it, baby," I murmur against her.

"I need you," she pants.

"Then say it." I nip the inside of her thigh and she jerks.

"Fuck my pussy with your mouth and do it now," she commands.

That a girl.

I eye her and bite down on the top of her panties, then slide them down with my teeth. She eagerly lifts her hips to aid my efforts and I use my hands to remove them the rest of the way.

"Jesus, baby. You're exquisite," I praise, my eyes gradually roaming over her gorgeous figure.

She groans. "Please, Chase."

"Shh, I got you." I place both of her legs up over my shoulders. I pin her hips down to the bed with my hands, spread her thighs open, and leisurely lick her pussy. She tastes even better than I imagined. I tease her by stopping for a moment and use my facial hair to tickle the inside of her thighs. I bring my fingers up to brush against the backs of her knees repeatedly. My hands travel up the backs of her legs, over her thighs, and her eyes flutter. I lift her hips to my mouth again, picking up right where I left off.

Just when I've fired her up enough to know she's experiencing uninhibited, unabashed pleasure, I circle her clit with my tongue and give her all I've got. She's gasping for air as I passionately hum and suck on her, sending vibrations up her body to drive her wild with need.

She's so raw and incredible. My dick is straining against my jeans and it's becoming painful now. I need to be inside of her but not before she finishes first. She's writhing and panting as I continue my oral assault. She loves it—every fucking minute of it. And so do I.

She grabs two handfuls of my hair and tightens up as a mouthful of expletives leave her lips in ecstasy. I press down on her clit to apply just the right amount of pressure she needs, and I moan hard one last time. That does the trick. She finds her release and comes forcefully.

She continues to writhe and convulse, but I don't stop tasting her. Her senses are in overdrive, and soon it will be too much stimulation to bear. When I've had my fill, I pull back and watch her continue to come undone. Then our eyes lock; her look is intense primal, swimming in pleasure. And it's in that moment that I realize, this woman fucking owns me.

ELEVEN

a m e l i a

I'm tingling everywhere. I don't know how else to explain it. My entire body is covered in goose bumps, and I feel light as a feather, like at any given moment, I could float away. My head is spinning, and my body feels like one giant puddle of sensation. I just experienced one of the hardest orgasms of my life, and the gorgeous man that gave it to me, is looking down at me like I'm a goddess that walks among men. It makes me feel powerful, desired.

The bed shifts as he places his hands on either side of my head, supporting his weight above me. His sapphire eyes bore into mine. I feel like he can see me exactly for who I am—inside and out. It's intense and unnerving, but for the first time in a very long time, I don't feel the need to hide from it. This is the part where, metaphorically, I reach into my chest, rip my heart out, and hand it over to Chase, praying he doesn't shatter it to pieces.

As if hearing my thoughts, he drops his face down so we're nose to nose, and then tilts his head to seal his mouth over mine. I take a deep breath and wind my arms around his neck, deepening the kiss. I slip my tongue into his mouth and taste him like I'm committing him to memory.

I use my strength to roll us over so that I'm straddling him. My damp hair falls in a dark curtain around my face, and I slowly run my hands up and down his chest. He raises a tattooed arm and pulls down on the straps of my shirt, exposing my black-lace bra. He takes a moment to enjoy the view before reaching around my back and dexterously unclasping it, freeing my breasts. The bra glides down my arms and falls to the bed. He sits up and tightly wraps his arms around my waist and tugs a hard nipple into his mouth. My head falls back and sharp sensations shoot off like fireworks down below.

I run my hands through his dark locks and grasp the hem of his shirt. He lifts his arms up and I drag it over his head. I stroke his face and kiss his lips, his cheek, and his temple. I push him back down onto his back and remove my shirt, which is bunched up around my stomach. I'm now completely naked and wet for him. I bend down and trail soft kisses up his torso. His skin is hard, yet smooth, beneath my lips.

His breathing is shallow. I can tell from the hard bulge in his pants, that he wants this as much as I do. I unbutton his jeans and slide the zipper down. Grabbing onto the sides, I attempt to pull them off, but fail miserably. *Figures.* Chuckling, he removes his wallet from his back pocket and sets it on the nightstand. He lifts his hips, allowing me to pull the jeans down. All that's left before me is him looking effortlessly sexy in a pair of black boxer briefs.

He startles me by latching onto my hips and abruptly rolling us, so he's on top again. His eyes darken in an instant. His mischievous look tells me that this small, tender moment between us, is over. He restrains my hands above my head as he skillfully rocks his hips into me. My body bows and begins to wind back up. I watch as his torso moves and flexes fluidly, each time he rubs up against me. It's a little teaser for what's to come. From what I can tell, I won't be disappointed.

"Do you have any idea how bad I want you?"

"I have an inkling." I quiver with pleasure when he rolls against me.

"You've been driving me crazy from day one. I knew you were different right off the bat, and when you so easily dismissed me, I knew I'd stop at nothing to get you."

"Stop at nothing to get me? Or to get me under you?" I tease. I know that Chase isn't in this solely for sex. If I even thought for one second, that he didn't genuinely like me, we wouldn't be in this position—literally.

"Baby, your quick wit is just as sexy and enticing as that gorgeous snatch between your legs," he says, flexing into me again. "But this conversation is over." He releases his hold on my hands and moves off the bed. He slides his boxer briefs down and grabs his wallet off of my nightstand. He pulls out a condom, rips the foil, and slides it on his impressive length, pumping himself a few times.

He walks up to the side of the bed, remains standing, and reaches out to grab my legs. "Get over here," he coaxes. In one swift tug, my body glides effortlessly across the sheets, right to him. My backside reaches the edge of the mattress and my legs dangle off the side. His hard erection slaps against the inside my thighs.

"Wrap your legs around me," he commands. I eagerly kick them up and lock them around his waist. He fists his cock in his hand and aligns it with my entrance. He teases me by sliding in just a fraction and pulling back out a few times. I'm slick, hot, and oh-so-ready for him. Without warning, he plunges deep inside of me—filling me to capacity.

Oh, God, he feels so good.

"Fuck, baby, you're so tight," he says, his voice strained. He carefully pulls back and slides inside me a couple more times, letting my body get used to him, or maybe calming himself down a little bit. I'm not sure which one.

"You okay?" he asks.

I nod. I'm more than okay, I'm flooded with euphoria. Overwhelming ecstasy. Chase is my addiction and I'm fiending. The way he makes me feel…I could never get enough of this, enough of him.

"Hang on to the sheets, baby. You're going to need them," he warns.

I spread my arms out and fist two handfuls of the sheets. He has a vice-like grip on my hips. He begins to move in and out of me, picking up his pace. I try to match him thrust for thrust, despite his almost painful hold on my hips. We find a perfect rhythm and both moan simultaneously as we continue our climb to the top.

He's pounding into me at a brutally delicious pace and I loudly praise him for it over and over again. He's fucking all of the pain, angst, and anger out of me. I'm right there with him every step of the way, willing it to never stop. After a while, we both start to sweat and pant from the workout.

Things take a different turn when he wraps his arm around my lower back and lifts me off the bed. He swings me around and roughly presses my back up against the nearest wall. He cages me with both of his forearms, my body being held up solely by the wall and my legs around him. I wrap my arms around his neck and tilt my head back, feeling his hot breath against my skin. His dark hair falls around his eyes and tickles my collarbone as he kisses my chest and neck furiously. My head is spinning, and each coming breath is more difficult to catch than the next.

"Look at me, Mia," he rasps.

I lower my head to look him in the eyes. He tightly grips my ass to support me and significantly slows his pace down to a deep, sensual thrust. My body calms down and switches gears to adapt, only to start winding back up. This is personal now, raw. The way he's looking into my eyes and gently thrusting in and out of me, it shows that he isn't just fucking me anymore.

"Grab onto my shoulders and take control while I hold you," he urges.

My hands run up the sides of his neck and back down to his shoulders, planting in place. I use the weight of his body to start sliding up and down his shaft as he holds me tight. With every stroke, he gently lifts me up to keep us in sync.

For the record, this position isn't as easy as it looks, folks.

I eventually find my own rhythm and stick with it. There's nowhere for me to escape or hide because he has me stripped down and completely exposed. I don't know which is more intimate: the fact that he's inside of me, or the affectionate way he's looking at me. My body begins to tighten and I know the end is near.

"Baby, I'm close," I whisper.

"I know. I can feel you tightening around my cock."

I need a little more momentum, so I move faster. He immediately takes the hint and thrusts harder, giving me exactly what I crave. Four pumps later, I'm coming again. I'm eternally grateful for the fact that he's holding me up because there's no way my legs would be able to support me right now. Watching me come undone must've triggered him. He lifts me up, slams me down to the base once more, and finds his own release.

"*Shit, Mia,*" he exalts.

We stand there, looking into each other's eyes and panting profusely. He slowly pulls out of me and I wince. Exhausted and emotionally spent, he walks us back to the bed and lies back down. We rest there together, his front to mine, and kiss each other reverently as our heart rates slow. The tingles are back in full force and I honestly don't have the energy to do anything but lay here and stare at him. His rough hands caress my back, and for once, I feel complete and utter peace.

He sits up, removes the condom, and leaves my room for a second to go clean himself up. I close my eyes and enjoy my temporary high. A minute or so later, he crawls back into bed. He pulls me into his arms and I rest my head on his chest. The last thing I remember before falling into a deep, sated sleep is him running his fingers through my damp hair.

• • •

I awake to the smell of bacon and the sound of pots and pans clattering against the stove. Mr. Tall, Dark, and Sinful is trailing soft kisses all the way up my spine. I keep my eyes closed and pretend to be asleep for a while longer so I don't distract him from this crucial task. He drops a final kiss between my shoulder blades, making me shiver. I open my eyes to find him looking down at me, adoringly. He nuzzles my cheek, his facial hair lightly scratching my skin.

"Wake up, gorgeous girl," he murmurs, sultry. His voice is extra deep and raspy this morning. It's delicious.

I groan and bury my face under my pillow to block out the light coming in through my window. He reaches under the sheet and pinches my side, making me squirm.

"Stop it, before I punch you in the throat," I say, my mouth muffled from the pillow.

"You're such a delight when you first wake up, you know that?"

I lift the pillow off my head and shoot him a stern look. He's fully dressed in last night's outfit and his hair is damp.

"I hope you don't mind, but I showered this morning and used your body wash. I highly doubt you'll be able to keep your hands off me now, not that you could before," he jokes.

I purse my lips to hide my smile and unabashedly pull the sheets off me, giving him an eyeful of my naked frame in broad daylight. If he's going to be cocky, then so will I. His gaze instantly moves down my body, and he looks like he just forgot whatever smartass comment he was going to make. *Excellent.* I bring my head up to my palm and rest my elbow against the bed.

"I'm sorry, you were saying?"

He's speechless. I smile with triumph.

"That's what I thought," I say, rolling off the bed. I grab my sweats off the floor and throw them on. I follow the delicious scent of bacon down the hall, leaving Chase still stunned in my room. I'm not sure what time Raven came home last night, but I'm about to find out.

I turn the corner. To my surprise, I see a naked broad back, and a head of blonde hair. There's Eric, standing in our kitchen, cooking breakfast, wearing only a pair of boxers. *So much for taking Sasha home….*

I feel Chase come up behind me and rest his palms on my hips. He leads us to the bar stools. Hearing us approach, Eric looks over his shoulder and gives us a beaming smile. He *definitely* got some last night.

Chase and I pull up a seat, and Eric sets two plates down in front of us.

"Morning. Y'all want some breakfast?"

"Yes, I'm starving," Chase replies.

"Me, too, please," I second that.

He grabs the skillet off the burner and serves us some scrambled eggs with cheese and peppers. He sets the pan back down on the burner, picks up a fork, and grabs us each a couple strips of bacon. I reach for my fork and dig in. It feels so good to eat something after last night's drinking and sexcapade. Eric grabs a mug and pours me a cup of coffee and sets the sugar next to it, knowing exactly how I like it. Just as I'm spooning some into my beverage, Raven emerges from her room.

"Smells delicious out here," she praises.

Eric catches her by the waist and pulls her into him. He cups her face and gives her a long, deep smooch on the lips. He releases her and shoves a cup of coffee in her hand, making her giggle.

"Thank you," she beams, taking a sip.

My life feels so surreal right now. I'm dying for some time with Raven to find out what went down last night after she left. Obviously it was something big, because the way she's acting this morning, is polar opposite of what we all experienced last night. If I wasn't so enthralled with Chase, I'd kick him out to find out what's going on. But, I think I'll keep him around for a little while longer...

"How'd you sleep, baby?" Eric asks her.

"I slept really well, pumpkin, thank you," Chase interjects.

Raven and I burst out laughing as Eric breaks off a piece of bacon and throws it at Chase.

"Hey, not in my kitchen," Raven scolds.

"Sorry, baby, I had to," Eric defends.

"So, what do you two have planned for today?" Raven asks, taking the focus off her and Eric.

"I'm not sure yet. I have to work at Surge tonight and I was going to ask Mia if she'd like to spend the day with me."

"Only if you let me drive your car," I reply.

"Excuse me?" He cocks an eyebrow.

"You heard me. I want to drive that car, and you promised me I could, remember?" I'm reminding him of the bet we made on our first date: the kiss in exchange for driving the Mustang. That first kiss had me so flustered that I forgot to cash in my end of the deal. Now, he's going to pay up.

He makes a low, guttural sound, but reluctantly agrees, and finishes off the last bite of his eggs. He knows I earned it fair and square, so he can't argue on this one.

After I finish my food, Chase stands up, takes our plates, and walks around to set them in the sink. He places both his hands down on the counter and leans over to kiss me.

"Go get ready so we can get out of here and have some fun."

He doesn't have to tell me twice.

Driving Chase's Mustang is such a thrill. I feel like a badass—like I've been reincarnated and I'm sixteen all over again. I'm cruising with the windows down, making this temporary rush feel even more monumental. The velvet, sultry vocals of Lana Del Rey are seeping through the speakers and keeping us company along the way. Chase is in the passenger's seat giving me heated eyes.

We aren't heading anywhere in particular. We're just enjoying the moment and seeing where the road takes us. That's one of the many things I admire about Chase—he has a carefree attitude and goes with the flow. Everything's so incredibly easy with him.

"Where'd you learn to drive a stick-shift?" he asks, breaking through the comfortable silence.

"My dad," I smile fondly at the memory. "When I was visiting him one summer, he took me out to the Hill Country area and taught me on a hill. It was quite the experience, let me tell you. I must've stalled the car fifteen times. I've never gotten the finger so many times in one day from other drivers. Towards the end, all I could smell was burnt clutch."

Chase physically cringes at the thought.

"Yeah, Dad was *super* thrilled. He was swearing up a storm the entire time. I told him he brought that one on himself. He's the one who insisted that I learn...on a hill, no less. Seriously, who does that?"

He laughs. "I'm impressed."

"Alright, your turn. How many tattoos do you have?" I noticed last night that he has some pieces on his back. They're all gorgeous, but I have no clue what any of them mean, if anything.

"Honestly, I lost count. Some of them have clashed to create one big one, but they were originally done as separate pieces, specifically the ones on my forearm."

"Do any of them have any special meaning?"

"A few. I have an angel on my right shoulder blade that's roping a heart. Megan has the same one in the same place. We got matching tattoos together for my twenty-first birthday. The angel means guardian or protector, the rope signifies the sibling bonds that tie us together, and the heart stands for love. In a roundabout way, it just means that we love each other, we're tied to each other, and we protect one another."

"That's so cool." I respect how close Chase is with his family. I honestly envy it. I remember feeling that way when my dad was still alive. It's one of the reasons why I wish I wasn't an only child. A part of me wants that sibling bond with someone, but at the same time, I'm glad I was it for my parents. I wouldn't want a sibling to have to live through the same childhood. Plus, it would have added an impossible task for me, financially. There's no way I could've worked two waitressing jobs and taken care of three people at nineteen. I was barely taking care of two.

Chase lifts my hand to his mouth, yanking me out of my reverie. He kisses the back, turns it over, and begins to brush his fingers along the inside of my palm. It's a welcome distraction that sends shivers up my spine.

"I really don't want to go into work tonight. I just want to stay here and do naughty things with you, all day and all night," he says wistfully.

I feel the same way, but I also don't want us to spend so much time together that we get sick of each other. But on the flipside, I also don't want to be apart from him for too long, either. I'm going to have to work on a healthy balance.

"I'm free Wednesday night," I offer an alternative.

"I'm free Wednesday night, too. After I get off work, do you want to come over and I'll cook us a meal?" he asks, hopeful. "Then maybe we can cuddle up on the couch naked and 'watch' movies together?"

"Is that all I'm good for now?" I feign insult.

"Mostly, yes," he laughs. "But in all seriousness, since I'm completely caught up in you and your amazing-ness, I guess you can call the shots," he appeases.

Feeling my heart race from that admission, I press down on the gas. The car lunges forward in an attempt to match the speed of my pounding heart. Off to the side, a bike rental stand catches my eye. It's been years since I've ridden a bike. Suddenly, I have the urge to be spontaneous and hit the trails with Chase. Before I miss my chance and drive past it, I hit the brakes and squeal into the parking lot. The bottom of the car accidently scrapes along the concrete when we go over a dip.

"Whoa, easy on my car, woman!" he barks.

"Babe, relax. I got this."

He shoots me a harsh look and shakes his head like he can't believe I talked him into driving his car.

"What are we doing here?"

I park the car and unbuckle my seatbelt. "We're going on a bike ride together."

His gaze cuts to mine and he raises an eyebrow. "Is that so?"

I nod enthusiastically. "Sure is. Raven, Eric, and I used to do this every summer when we were teenagers, before any of us had cars. Anywhere we went, we were on bikes. Come on, it'll be fun."

Without responding, he hops out, shuts the door a little harder than necessary, and walks around to the front, leaving me inside. He bends down and looks underneath, assessing the damage. I wait anxiously and bite down on my fingernails, preparing for the worst.

He stands up straight and glares at me through the windshield. *Oh, crap.* I slowly open the door and crawl outside like a puppy with its tail between its legs.

"You are so lucky, you know that?"

My face falls. "Lucky that you like me, or lucky because there's no damage?"

"Oh, it's definitely scratched, just not as bad as I thought it would be."

"I'm so sorry. I promise, I'll make it up to you."

He crosses his arms over his chest. "How can you possibly make it up to me?"

I take a moment to think that one over.

Shit.

Wait a minute...I've got it!

"I'll let you drive me to the middle of nowhere and fuck me on the hood," I suggest.

"*That's* what you're bargaining with? Sex?"

"Don't rule it out yet. Just picture it: the two of us out in the country together, under the scorching Texas sun, going at it on top of your car without a care in the world." I walk around and place my hands down on the hood, then pop my backside out. "Oh, baby—ah, that's hot!" I jump back and shake my hands.

Chase is trying hard to suppress a smirk.

"Okay, so maybe not on the hood in the Texas heat. How about the backseat?" I recover.

He drops his arms and walks over to where I'm standing. He reaches out and grabs my face. "Babe?"

Reluctantly, I look up at him. "Yeah?"

"You didn't scratch the car."

My eyes widen and I push at his chest. "Oh, my God. Are you serious?!"

He stumbles backwards and throws his head back, roaring with laughter. "You should've seen your face. Fucking priceless."

"You jerk! I almost had a heart attack. You even had me trading in sexual favors to make it right!" I shout.

"No, Mia, that was *all* you," he holds up his hands defensively.

"I'm so mad at you right now."

"It's okay, I'll make it up to you on the hood of my car," he bursts out laughing again. I feel a raging fire spread inside me and I turn to walk away.

"Hey, wait up!" he calls after me.

I ignore him and pick up the pace. He charges me from behind, wraps his arms around me, and lifts me off the ground.

"Put me down!" I try to wrestle out of his hold.

He sets me down on my feet, dips me low, and kisses me hard on the mouth before I have a chance to yell at him. Caught off guard, I freeze, then slowly close my eyes and wind my arms around his neck. He brings us both back up and breaks the lip-lock.

"You're beautiful," he murmurs, stroking my nose with his. "I'm one lucky son of a bitch."

I feel my anger evaporate and I soften in his arms. "You. Me. A bike ride?"

"Done." He casually wraps his arm around my shoulders and walks us over to the rental stand.

We spend the next two hours racing through Barton Springs. It's warm out, but the trees are doing a decent job of shading us. I feel just as wild and untamed as these rocky trails we're conquering together. Chase seems to think he's a BMX star, performing small jumps and tricks every now and then, keeping me on my toes. *Showoff. Pssh, whatever.* As much as I hate to admit it, he's actually good. He's stupid awesome. There's really no use in denying or fighting it anymore; I'm falling for him.

TWELVE

c h a s e

’ll admit, I’m not the world’s greatest cook, but I’m trying. I don’t know what the hell I was thinking when I offered to cook her dinner. It sounded like a great idea in theory, but in practice it’s quickly turning into an impossible task. I’m not even making anything that complex—bow-tie pasta with a creamy wild mushroom sauce, baked potatoes, and a side salad. What’s throwing me off? All the damn multitasking it takes to make this stuff. But have no fear; I have a backup plan if things go bust—Chinese takeout.

It’s the thought that counts, right?

The good news is that I chose a pretty good wine to go with our food tonight, and I’ve lit candles—all over the living room and kitchen table—making my apartment feel romantic. It’s almost six-thirty, which means Mia will be here any minute. I pull the baked potatoes out of the oven to let them cool down and grab two wine glasses from the cupboard. I pour the wine, screw the cork back on the bottle, and pace around the kitchen nervously, waiting for the sauce to finish heating up. I focus on keeping myself busy and set the table with two plates, napkins, and all the utensils we'll need. It's right then that I hear a knock, but before I get a chance to walk over to the door, it opens and closes.

"Ooh, it smells good in here," a female voice praises, but it's not Mia's.

Megan walks over and sets her purse down on the couch. She wanders into the kitchen, her heels striking the tile floor, and leans over the stove to take a whiff of the sauce.

"It's definitely the candles," she concludes.

"Shit, Meg, don't tell me that."

She comes up and puts an arm around my back and pulls me into a side hug. "Lighten up, I'm only kidding. The food smells delicious. Need any help?"

"No, what I need is for you to leave before Mia gets here."

She swings around, grabs a glass, and starts to pour herself some water from the fridge, making herself at home.

"Meg, I'm not kidding. You need to leave, like now."

"But, I want to meet her," she presses.

"No. The last thing I want is for this date to turn into a family affair. We're still getting to know each other and I don't want her to feel uncomfortable because my older sister is around. I don't want to feed her to the wolves."

Meg scoffs and takes a sip of her water. "I'm hardly a wolf, Chase. Just because I didn't like Christa doesn't mean I won't like Mia. I'm sure she's a completely different type of girl. It's nice to see someone get under your skin for a change. Based on that, I already like her."

I turn the stove off, reach for the sauce, and take it off the burner. I carefully pour it into the bowl with the pasta and stir it all up. One by one, I set each dish down on the kitchen table for us to self-serve. Three loud raps echo throughout the apartment and Meg quickly sets her glass down and races to the front door, beating me there. Highly impatient, she opens it, and there stands Mia on the other side. She looks breathtaking like always. She's wearing a turquoise T-shirt, dark blue jeans, and brown cowgirl boots.

I stand next to Megan, completely captivated. Mia looks between Meg and I, uncomfortable—and, if I'm not mistaken, maybe even a little hurt. She shifts back and forth on her feet and tucks an invisible strand of hair behind her ear. She looks up at me with a frown. Oh shit, she's getting the wrong idea. I clear my throat and push the door open wider, out of Meg's hold, and stand off to the side, silently inviting Mia in. Reluctantly, she steps inside and takes a rigid stance on the opposite side of us.

"Amelia, this is my sister, Megan. Meg, this is Mia, my girlfriend."

Mia looks at me with a hint of surprise—or maybe shock—but then composes herself and relaxes. Her guarded expression is replaced with a friendly smile as she extends her hand.

Meg grasps it and returns her smile.

"Nice to meet you, Mia. I've heard a lot about you," she says politely.

"It's great to meet you, too. Chase has told me a lot about you as well."

Meg looks at me and raises her brows. "Is that right?"

"All good things," I reassure her.

"Good." She walks over to the couch to retrieve her purse and strides back over to the door. She pulls me into a goodbye hug, then turns and regards Mia warmly. "It was nice to meet you, Mia. Maybe I'll get to see you again soon and we can get to know each other a little better," she suggests.

"I'd love that," Mia says with sincerity.

Meg steps out and turns around to face us. "You two enjoy your evening, and Mia, don't be surprised if his cooking is awful. He can't cook to save his life, but on the flipside, he makes great furniture—so I guess it all balances out. Either way, you've been warned."

Mia laughs. I could seriously strangle Meg for that comment. I know she means well, but I've stressed about it enough and she knows that.

"Bye, Meg," I say too loudly and start to close the door. I see her grin and walk off right before it closes. I lock the door and turn around to face Mia.

"Your sister seems really nice."

"She's a pain in the ass." I saunter toward her. With Mia looking that gorgeous, I'm done talking about my sister. She automatically takes a few steps back to widen the space between us. I pick up my pace and fill it. The backs of her legs meet the back of my couch and stop her from going any farther. Our bodies are barely touching, but her chest is lightly brushing up against mine with each breath she takes. I can tell from the look on her face that she wants to say something, but she hesitates. I stroke her forehead with the tips of my fingers, moving her side-swept bangs out of her eye. She reaches up and grasps both of my arms, closes her eyes, and leans forward to inhale my scent.

She makes a satisfied little noise in the back of her throat and opens her eyes to capture my gaze. Seconds, minutes, maybe hours tick by as we continue to just stare at each other. Tilting my head to the side, I reach up to cup both of her cheeks in my hands, my thumbs stroking her cheeks. Her skin is always so soft and smooth.

"What's on your mind, baby?" I ask softly.

"Nothing," she says dismissively.

"Tell me."

She chews her bottom lip in contemplation. "It's just...you introduced me as your girlfriend."

"Yeah, so?" I say, not understanding the point. "Did that bother you?"

"No, not at all. I'm just confused as to whether you said that because your sister was standing there, or because you actually feel that way about us. I mean, I know you like me, don't get me wrong, but I also know that you don't really do the whole girlfriend thing. I guess it just caught me off guard, that's all."

I reach down to grab her hands and intertwine our fingers together and take a small step back, my stance becoming more serious.

"Mia, I'm kind of crazy about you. After spending the last couple of nights together, I don't want to share you with anyone else, and I certainly don't want to stop seeing you. I told you before, you're more than just a fling. I value and respect you. When I feel this way about a woman, I give her the commitment she deserves. So whether you like it or not, you have me." And then I can't help myself. "You get no say in this, so just bend over and take it."

Her mouth falls open in mock horror and she rips her hand from mine. She pinches me hard on my side, I jump back in defense and laugh loudly, my voice traveling throughout the room. When she figures out that I'm ticklish, she goes in for the kill as I try to fight her off. After a few seconds, she steps back and eyes me sternly.

"Take it back. Right now," she demands.

"Absolutely not," I defy.

She steps forward and starts tickling me again, mercilessly, as I roar with laughter. "Fine, then *you* bend over and take it," she counters. I seize one of her arms but she gets me with the other one.

"Okay! Okay!" I hold my hands up and surrender.

"So, you take it back?" she asks.

"Yes, I take it back. After spending the last few nights together, I think we should see other people. You are no more than a fling to me, and I don't have an ounce of feeling for you whatsoever. No matter how hard you beg, you'll never be my girlfriend. So quit being so desperate and—"

She grabs my face and smashes her lips to mine, cutting off my unromantic declaration. I wrap my arms around her back, squeezing the hell out of her. After a few moments, I break the kiss before I'm in too deep.

"Come on, let's eat. The food's going to get cold and I put a lot of effort into making it. Plus, I'm fucking starving, and if you keep kissing me that way, I'll be eating something other than food, and that's supposed to be for dessert."

Grabbing her hand, I lead us toward the kitchen table. I pull her chair out, and she takes a seat, scooching herself in as I grab our glasses of wine off the counter.

"Everything looks really good," she says, placing her napkin in her lap.

"There are no guarantees," I warn. "My sister was pretty spot-on when she made those comments."

"I'm sure it will taste fine," she reassures.

"Well, don't hold back. Dig in."

I sit down and take my own advice after Mia finishes filling her plate. We spend the better part of dinner delving into deeper topics. We talk about everything from societal issues, to our personal goals and aspirations, to our family life. The wine is helping us philosophize, and it also seems to be bringing out the more opinionated side of Mia. When she says things, she says them with a strong conviction, standing by her reasoning. She's not close-minded or arrogant about it, just passionate. It's quite a turn-on.

I'm discussing things with her that I've never discussed with any woman other than Meg. As I sit here and eat my pasta, I listen attentively to what she's saying and try not to focus too much on her body language. I do pick up on the way her cheeks flush when we butt heads on a topic, and how she uses her hands to animatedly describe what she's trying to say, and how when she's deep in thought, her fingers circle the bowl of the wine glass absentmindedly. I love how her nose scrunches up when she giggles at something I say, and how witty she can be in general. When I dish it out, she gives it right back.

The food didn't turn out so bad after all. Both of us had room for seconds, finishing off almost everything I made, and we drained the bottle of wine. The sun has set outside so there's no more natural light coming in through the windows, just candlelight everywhere. I'm not the most romantic guy, but I'm going to give myself points for this one (and I think you probably should, too.) The effort was made, I'm behaving like a gentleman, nothing went wrong.

Mia excuses herself to the bathroom and I begin to clean up all of the dishes. Her phone lights up and vibrates on the table with an incoming call. I ignore it and keep washing plates. It lights up and vibrates again. I'm tempted to answer it this time, but I don't want her to get pissed and think I'm screening her calls. That's not my style. I look at the phone and see that it's her mom calling. I set it back down and mind my own business. Then she calls a third time. Figuring that it might be an emergency, my curiosity gets the better of me and I slide my finger across the screen to answer.

"Mia's phone, Chase speaking."

"Who the hell is this?" a sharp voice bites through the speaker.

"I'm Mia's boyfriend," I say casually.

"You're telling me that my daughter has only been down there for a couple weeks and already she has a boyfriend? What, did her legs just fall open?"

I'm completely taken aback. I have no idea how to handle this woman, and I can't believe she just said that about her own daughter. Mia steps out of the bathroom and waltzes into the living room.

When she notices my shocked expression, her brows furrow in confusion. Her mother continues to rant on the other end.

"What's the matter, Chaaaase?" she slurs. "Cat got your tongue? Or does Mia have it?"

Mia's eyes widen in horror and all the blood drains from her face. She looks paralyzed, unable to move a muscle or even breathe.

"Uh, Nancy? I think Mia's going to have to call you back later," I say, unsure.

"Put her on the phone! That little shit owes me money!"

Before I have a chance to tell Nancy to go fist herself, Mia snaps out of her trance and grabs the phone out of my hand. "What do you want?" she asks harshly.

I can hear yelling on the other end, but between the slurring and the endless run-on sentences, I can't decipher what she's saying. I keep my eyes trained on Mia.

"Mom, I'm not paying that, again; we've gone over this," Mia says, forcing herself to stay calm.

The shouting continues, and Mia looks into my eyes, pissed. "Mom, we've been over this. I'm not going to pay the house bill and I'm not coming back home. If you call me one more time," she grits, "I'll file harassment charges. You got that...you little shit?" She ends the call, slams the phone down, and lets out a shaky breath, using the counter to hold herself steady.

I give her a minute to calm down before I explain myself. She looks up and studies me, a frown marring her beautiful features.

"Why would you answer my phone?" she asks sharply.

And cue the groveling....

"I'm sorry, that wasn't what it seemed like. I swear, I wasn't trying to screen your calls or snoop around. I was cleaning up while you were in the bathroom when I saw your mom call numerous times. I thought maybe it was important, but I shouldn't have done that. I'm an idiot. Forgive me?" I ask, sincere and hopeful.

When you've been in hot water as many times as I have, you become accustomed to these types of situations. Thankfully, I know all the right things to say and do in order to get myself out. Goes along with my charm.

She lets out a weary sigh and her shoulders sag, making me feel even worse. I walk around and pull her into my arms, attempting to make it right. She's trembling, but I'm not sure if it's from fear or anger. I rub my hands up and down her arms for comfort, but it doesn't stop the tears from welling up in her eyes.

"Shh, it's okay, baby," I soothe.

"No, it's not okay. I'm so sorry for the things she said to you," she sniffs.

I try for humor. "Don't apologize. It's my fault. I'm the idiot who thought it'd be cute to say hi to your mom—like when my sis crashed our party earlier just to meet you." And then I add, "And you can't own her actions and mistakes like they're yours. Understand?"

"I can't help it," she sobs.

I lift her up and carry her down the hall into my bedroom, gently laying her down on my bed. I reach out to turn on the lamp, and the room warms with light. I crawl in behind her, fold my arms around her, and hold on while she cries. I knew she had issues with her mother, but I had no idea it was this bad. No wonder Mia left.

"Are you okay?" I have no clue how much time has passed, but we've been in here for a while.

Mia turns onto her back and looks at me. Her nose is red and her eyes are puffy. "Yeah, I think so," she says hoarsely. I caress her jaw, searching for any sign to indicate how she's truly feeling.

"We don't have to talk about this if you don't want to, but I want to know, how long has this been going on?"

She lets out a heavy sigh and uses her hands to push herself up into a sitting position. I follow her cue and do the same so we're sitting face-to-face. Knowing that this is a vulnerable moment for her, and a tough subject, I give her my full attention.

"It started becoming a habit when I was around fifteen, but it didn't get really bad until my dad died three years ago. His death sent her into a tailspin. It sent us both into a tailspin, she just never came out of it. Suddenly, the life that I'd always known slipped right through my fingers, like quicksand. My mom started to fall behind on the bills and couldn't catch up because she couldn't hold down a job. She'd either show up drunk, hung-over, or not at all. She was constantly getting fired. We were going to lose the house if we didn't do something, so I dropped out of college and picked up a second job to help out. By that point, she'd amassed so much debt, there was no way I was going to be able to completely pull us out from under, but at least I was making payments on the house again, so the bank backed off. I was working myself into the ground and giving up my life. She's a slave to her drinking, and because I was living under the same roof and taking care of us, I was a slave to her drinking, too. That thought scared me to death. I saw the next forty years flash by and I pictured myself in the exact same place. It just felt like it was never going to end unless I did something to change my situation."

"So that's why you left and came here?" I ask.

She nods. "We ended up getting into a huge fight one night before I left town. I gave a week's notice at both jobs, packed my bags, and stayed with Hadley while I finished out the remainder of my shifts. I called my mom and told her I was leaving to come down here, but I don't think she actually believed me at the time. She's been trying to pressure me into coming back home and giving her money ever since."

"Do you feel guilty for leaving. Like you made the wrong decision?"

She ponders my question.

"Sometimes," she admits. "It's hard. Deep down, I know I made the right choice, but it's not easy feeling like I'm letting her down. She's still my parent and I don't want anything to happen to her. I feel like if something goes wrong and I'm not there, it will be my fault. It's not like she has anybody to call for help, not that she would try anyway. She's completely alienated herself from everyone who cares about her."

I bring my finger under her chin and tilt her head up so she's looking me in the eyes. "You made the right choice, Mia. You can only do so much to save somebody. At the end of the day, if they don't want to be saved, then there's nothing you can do. I know it's hard, but you have to accept that. Better for her to fall down on her own, than to go down and take you with her," I say gently.

She snorts and rolls her eyes. "You sound like my therapist," she says with a hint of humor.

I give her a sympathetic smile and push a loose tendril of hair behind her ear. "I'm sorry that you have to put up with this, but you have to know it's not supposed to be that way for a kid, right? Children shouldn't have to make those kinds of sacrifices in order to take care of their parents, and they shouldn't be attacked by them, either."

"I know. She didn't used to be that way. She was actually a really great mom. She would always read me stories before bed and snuggle with me when I had nightmares. Whenever I was in a school play, she'd be front and center with a camera in one hand and a tissue in the other," she says nostalgically. "But all of that seems like it happened another lifetime ago," she adds, her tone sad and wistful.

Knowing what she's had to endure these last few years makes my heart ache for her. I want to kiss away her pain, healing every wound she's ever had. I want to wrap my arms around her and shield her from all the bullshit life has to offer. I know she can take care of herself, but she shouldn't have to. She's already done enough of that.

Her openness and vulnerability are tugging on my protective instincts, and I suddenly feel an itch to hold her. I grab her waist and pull her on top of my lap. She straddles me and runs her fingers through my hair. Her touch feels so comforting. I close my eyes and let my head fall back in contentment. Soft kisses fall on my face and I groan. As she continues down to my throat, I knead her hips. Mia pulls back and I open my eyes.

"Chase?" she says softly.

"What do you need, baby?" I ask, already knowing where she's going with this.

"You," she breathes.

"You've got me."

I lean forward, forcing her body backward until she's lying down on the bed again. I give her slow, exaggerated kisses and shift my weight so only my forearms are holding me up. Her small body feels perfect under mine. She wraps her legs around me and my hand slides from her ankle all the way up to her thigh. Feeling the texture of her cowgirl boots against my skin reminds me of a thought I previously had and I break the kiss.

"I want you to close your eyes. Then, I'm going to slide your clothes off your body until I have you completely naked. Once I've done that, I'm going to take all this shit away for you. And you know what you're going to be wearing while I do that?" I say.

"Nothing?"

"Close. You'll be wearing nothing but these boots...and me," I vow.

A slow smile spreads across her face as I lean back down and begin to fulfill my promise.

By the time the night is over, I've fulfilled it three times.

THIRTEEN

It's been almost six weeks since I last heard from my mom, but I'm not complaining. I'm enjoying the silence and letting things come together, which is enabling me to fall into a welcome routine. I started my job at the steakhouse a few weeks ago, and I'm absolutely loving it. It's fast paced, fun, and the people there are great to work with.

Chase and I are doing fantastic, but work has been keeping both of us busy, so we don't see each other as often as we'd like. When he found out I'd gotten the job, he took me zip lining to celebrate. Little did I know, it was also his way of making me take a risk and try something new.

As for Raven and Eric, they've been inseparable, spending almost every night together at his place for the last week. It turns out that the two of them got together shortly before I moved down. After several miscommunications, and stubbornly refusing to tell each other how they felt, they finally got on the same page.

This brings us to today—it's Thanksgiving. Raven and I are cooking the stuffing and sweet potatoes. When I say "we're" cooking, that really means she's doing all the work while I sit on top of the counter and keep her company. Let's face it, there's no way she would ever let me touch such a high-profile dinner. Since I have nowhere to go for the holidays, she invited me to her parents' house, and I accepted. Chase invited me to do dinner with his family, too, but after an intense conversation, and a long list of reasons why it's too soon to meet his entire family, he relented.

"Mia, can you hand me that large Tupperware sitting next to you?"

"Of course," I say, reaching over to grab it. "What's the update with you and Eric? You guys seem to be pretty hot and heavy lately."

"Things are good," she says, contentedly. "I think it helps that we were friends for so long first. I know a lot of people think he's a vapid man-whore, but I see past that stupid exterior. He can't fool me."

"I can't believe I didn't see what was going on. I feel like I should've known all along. I'm losing my edge and I blame Chase for that," I half joke.

"No, you aren't. We were really good at keeping it hidden and, to be honest, there wasn't really anything to tell."

"Yeah, but you liked him, and you didn't tell me. I know it's not my business, but that kind of surprised me. I tell you everything. I'd be lying if I said it didn't sting that you never mentioned anything," I say, feeling a little wounded.

She sets the container of stuffing down and exhales. "I'm sorry. I wasn't trying to hide anything from you. But I also didn't want you to be put in the middle of our drama. I wasn't going to say anything until we figured our situation out, but when I saw him with Sasha at ACL, I just couldn't hold it in any longer."

"How long have you liked him?"

She takes a moment to think. "Probably for a year or so," she admits, guilty.

"A *year*?! And you didn't say anything to me? God, I feel like such a bad friend." And that's when I realize what's really bothering me. It's not that fact that she didn't tell me, and it's not necessarily that I didn't see it coming, it's that I feel like I wasn't there for her when she's always made a point to be there for me.

"Stop, don't even think like that, Mia. You've been nothing but supportive. It wasn't because I felt like I couldn't talk to you. You're my best friend. I've never felt like I had an issue that I couldn't talk to you about," she says adamantly.

Hearing her say that makes me feel a little bit better. She moves to the edge of the counter and pulls me into a tight hug. I hug her back fiercely and try to shake this feeling of not being good enough.

"You know that I'm really happy for you, right?" I ask, releasing her.

"I know, and I love you for it, baby girl." She gives me a grateful smile and returns to scooping the stuffing into the Tupperware. I hop down off the counter to grab our coats out of the closet. Now that it's well into November, it's gotten cold outside. However, I emphasize "cold" loosely because it's not nearly as frigid as the Midwest.

I shrug my coat on and hand Raven hers, then grab the stuffing and bottle of wine I purchased as a *thank you* to her parents for letting me spend Thanksgiving with them. Raven said it wasn't necessary, but I'd insisted. If there's one thing her mom can't resist, it's a good bottle of wine.

The timer goes off while she's slipping her coat on. She throws on the oven mitts, grabs the casserole dish, and closes the door with her foot. She tears off a sheet of aluminum foil and covers the sweet potatoes, being careful not to burn herself in the process. I switch off all the knobs, and do a quick sweep throughout the apartment to make sure all the lights are off. Raven walks out the front door with the dish while I lock up and briskly follow her to the car. For most of the ride there, I can't help but think about the bittersweet details of my last good Thanksgiving.

Five Years Earlier…

A shrill noise wakes me up from a deep sleep. Somewhere far off in my hazy mind, I recognize it as the smoke detector. Startled, I bolt upright and look around the room frantically. There's a powerful dose of smoke filling the house, which only makes my heart do double time. I throw the covers back and sprint out my room and down the hall to find the source.

"Dad!" I shout, panicked.

"In here!" he yells from the kitchen.

I swing around the corner in record speed and see Dad waving a frying pan right below the smoke detector to shut it up. *It's too early for this.* There's a visible cloud of smoke in the room, which is coming directly from the oven.

"What happened?" I yell over the noise.

"Burnt the damn turkey," he says, flustered.

I crank the kitchen window open, helping to air the smoke out. When the beeping finally stops, we relax and stare at each other for a long moment. My dad looks tired and depleted. He's dressed in a stained, gray T-shirt, a flannel, and dark jeans. There's a five o'clock shadow on his face and it's 10:00 a.m. I break eye contact to glance at the turkey. It's completely destroyed. My dad follows my line of vision and his shoulders slump.

"I'm sorry, kiddo. I didn't mean to ruin Thanksgiving for you."

"It's okay, Dad," I reassure, forcing my tone to sound lighthearted.

He sighs. "No, it isn't. This is the first Thanksgiving I've gotten to spend with you in a long time, and I can't even get the damn turkey right."

My hand flies up to cover my mouth and a chuckle escapes despite my best efforts. His eyes flicker to mine, confused at first, but then they soften.

He looks back over at the turkey—which is crisp and *way* too dark to eat. "Eh, it doesn't look so bad, does it?"

"Looks absolutely delicious."

He cracks a smile and grabs the corner of his T-shirt, lifting it to wipe the sweat off his forehead. "How does KFC sound? We can get a bucket of crispy chicken to share, mashed potatoes and gravy, some corn. That covers all the basics, right? I mean, I know your mom cooks all those things and more for you every year, and I'm fully aware her cooking is a whole lot better than fast food, but it's the best idea I've got."

I swallow hard and force myself to block out the problems I'm having back home. *Mom cooking a meal? Celebrating traditions like we used to? Sure, we'll go with that.*

"Are they even open today?" I ask, distracting myself.

"They sure are."

I study his smirk long enough to "get it." KFC has been his version of Thanksgiving dinner for years. It makes me sad to think that he usually does this all on his own. I don't want him to get lonely down here, living so far away from us.

"Only if you get me a side of mac 'n' cheese, too," I bargain.

He walks over and throws an arm around the back of my neck. "You got it, kiddo."

We shower and cruise to grab our replacement meal. Then we sit on the couch together and eat it. I mean, without a formal turkey dinner, why sit at the kitchen table, right? Dad jumps up and puts on his favorite Beatles album, then hops back on the couch. He looked like a kid at Christmas there for a second, so excited and animated.

"How's school going?" he asks, taking a bite of chicken.

"It's high school, Dad. It only gets so good."

"Hey, you're only a kid once. Don't forget that. You should at least try to make the most of it while you can. Are your grades still doing well?"

"Define 'well.'"

He shoots me a stern look. "You better not be letting your grades slip."

"Dad…"

"I'm serious. You need to focus on school. You still want to go to college, don't you?"

"Of course."

"Then buckle down."

"It's not like they're suffering or anything," I mutter.

"I don't care. It's obviously not your best work. Your mother and I don't expect all straight A's, but we do expect that you work hard and give one hundred percent. You're not giving it your best effort," he says matter-of-factly.

"Can we not talk about this, please?" I just want to enjoy my time with him and not think about home or school. I'm already dreading my inevitable return to Mom. He has no clue what's going on, and the longer we talk about this stuff, the harder it will be not to break down and tell him everything. There's no sense in making him feel guilty for something he can't change. I'm already doing that enough for the both of us.

Noticing the shift in my mood, he sets his chicken down and looks at me with concern. "What's going on with you?"

"Nothing," I lie. "I promise I'll do better in school if that's what you want, but I don't want to talk about this anymore. I don't get to see you as often as I'd like, and I want to make the most of our time before I have to fly back home."

He wipes the grease off his hands with a paper towel. "Should I be worried about something?"

"Not at all. Why do you ask?"

"Because you're not acting like yourself, that's why."

"I just have a lot on my mind lately. College, boys, life...you know, the usual stuff." I say vaguely.

"Boys? What boys?" he asks, alarmed.

"Relax, Dad. It's nothing serious."

"Better not be," he mutters. "You're too young for boys."

"I'm seventeen," I remind him.

"Exactly. You're too young. You don't need to waste your time dating when no one's good enough for you."

"And what exactly constitutes as being good enough?"

"Definitely not seventeen-year-old boys. Let's just leave it at that. Wait for someone who is actually worth your time. You'll know what I'm talking about when you find it—someday *far* away from now."

I roll my eyes. "I think you're being a tad overprotective."

"That's it? I was aiming for suffocating. Thought I'd achieved it when I saw the eye roll, too." He nudges me with his elbow.

I smile and lean in to rest my head against his bicep.

He stares down at me for a moment or so before the song changes to "Dear Prudence." Abruptly, he stands up and motions for me to do the same. I grab the paper towel he used and wipe my own hands off, then follow suit. He leads me to the middle of the living room. Knowing exactly what comes next, I drape my arm across the backs his shoulders and take his left hand in my right. His fingers curl around my hand and he wraps his other arm around my waist. He begins to sway us to the music, his eyes twinkling with pride. He spins me around as the rhythm picks up, and dips me low to the ground, causing me to giggle.

"You're my favorite daughter," he admits, bringing me back up.

"I'm your only daughter."

"Yeah, but you're still my favorite."

"Thanks."

"I mean it," his says, his face going completely serious. "You're a good kid, Mia, and you've got such a good head on your shoulders. You make me proud."

"I'm not really a kid anymore."

"I know," he says nostalgically, his eyes sad. "But you'll always be my little girl. No matter how old you get, that never changes."

"Ugh, why are you getting all sentimental?" I feign exasperation.

He laughs, twirls me around, and pulls me back in. "What do you want me to say? It's the holidays and, for once, it's my turn to have you. Sorry for cramping your style."

"Oh, my God, please stop. This is getting weird."

He lifts me off the ground, making exaggerated noises in the process—as if I weigh a thousand pounds. I wrap my arms around his neck and he gives me the biggest bear hug.

"Dad...can't...breathe."

He sets me back down on my feet and releases me.

"Hey, do me a favor and help your old man clean all this stuff up, will ya?" He motions his head in the direction of the coffee table. I nod and walk over. We start stacking dishes, one by one. I stop for a brief second, taking a moment to appreciate him.

"Hey, Dad?"

He looks up at me.

"Thanks for the food. It's been an awesome day."

He smiles. "You're welcome, kiddo."

Unforgettable is what that was. Dad had initially felt bad for what had happened with the turkey; said something about 450 degrees looking like 250 in the middle of the night in low light. Shit happens, is what I told him. He seemed to shake off the disappointment after that.

Eating a turkey didn't make that Thanksgiving special, seeing him did. My dad, a bucket of KFC, and The Beatles rocked that holiday. Best Thanksgiving ever.

The celebration with Raven's family tonight came in second, though, a close second. I can't believe how safe and loved I felt. It's easy to forget how fulfilling that time can be when you have no real family left. Each and every person was so warm and inviting, and the food was fantastic. Her mom even sent us both home with a big bag of leftovers. *Score!*

Acting solely on my good mood, I pull out my phone and just for a moment, I'm tempted to text my mom and wish her a Happy Thanksgiving. I'm staring at her name on my screen with the option to call a click away, but I change my mind at the last second. She's like a shark; when she smells blood, she strikes.

Suddenly, my phone lights up and vibrates, startling me.

Chase: *How was your Thanksgiving? Did you miss me?*

Don't smile, don't smile, don't smile. Dammit, I'm smiling. I quickly type out a response, choosing to be playful.

Me: *Our Thanksgiving was awesome. As far as missing you, not really…*

It only takes him about ten seconds to respond.

Chase: *Yeah, I didn't really miss you either. It was nice to finally have a break from your overbearing neediness and constant whining.*

I laugh, and Raven looks over at me. When we come to the stop sign ahead, I use the free moment to show her the text he sent. She smiles and shakes her head, clearly not getting it. "Y'all are so weird."

She continues to drive, while I get back to texting Chase.

Me: *Whatever, all my other boyfriends keep telling me I'm the "ideal" girlfriend. Whatever that means.*

I press send.

Chase: *They're just saying that to get into your pants. Ditch those losers and come spend the night with me instead. I promise, I'll make it worth your while.*

Me: *Really? Do tell.*

Chase: *Come over here and I'll show you…*

I take a couple minutes to think that one over—to keep him on the edge of his seat more than anything else. When I'm satisfied with the amount of time that's elapsed, I give him a response.

Me: *As soon as we get back to our place, I'll head over.*

Chase: *Excellent choice, baby :).*

Smiling, I lean my head back against the headrest and stare out the window. My thoughts drift to how much Chase has done for me, without him even realizing it. I'll admit, when I first met him, I thought there was no way that anything would work between us, but he's pleasantly surprised me. Who knew he could be so incredibly funny, brutally honest, and wonderfully irresistible? He brings out my fun side, but at the same time, he anchors me. He helps me see what I'm capable of achieving and how strong I really am, even though I don't always feel that way. I like to think that he feels the same way about me, because honestly, I'm in too deep now. If this relationship ends badly, there's no way I'll be able to repair the damage to my heart. And that thought is daunting.

FOURTEEN

c h a s e

’m taking the day off for a change. I have plenty of vacation time built up, and for once, I have a good reason to use it. I already texted Raven to see if Mia's home, and she told me she is. I thought it'd be a good idea to surprise her and spend the day together. She works tonight, but at least this way, I'll get to see her before her shift starts. Unfortunately, due to our work schedules, I won't get a chance to see her again for the next couple of days.

I stop at Starbucks on the way to her apartment and order a pumpkin spiced latté for her, and a medium roast coffee for me.

(And you thought I was only useful for my striking looks...shame on you.)

Once I reach the front door, I balance her coffee on top of mine and let myself in. I asked Raven to leave it unlocked when she left to go study for her finals this morning. It's early, so I'm hoping Mia's still asleep. I quietly walk down the hall, not bothering to take my shoes off because Raven isn't here to yell at me. I slowly turn Mia's doorknob, careful not to make a sound. I open the door to find her sleeping on her stomach—arms and legs sprawled out across the mattress. She's wearing a snug, white tee, and a pair of polka dotted underwear.

Fuck. Yes.

I set the coffee cups down on her nightstand, and gently crawl onto the bed, being extra careful not to wake her. I watch her sleep soundly for a few minutes, taking her in and enjoying the view. My fingers reach out and trace her back.

She lets out a small moan and stirs. I bring my lips to her ear and whisper, "Good morning, baby." Her eyes pop open with a hint of alarm, but once she realizes it's me, she relaxes. Rolling over to face me, I'm greeted with a spectacular view of her nipples through her shirt.

"What time is it?" she asks groggily.

"A little after eight."

She lets out a frustrated groan and drops her head back down on the pillow, making me chuckle. My girl is definitely not a morning person.

"Why are you here so early?" she whines.

"I brought you nourishment." I grab her cup off the nightstand and wave the opening of the lid below her nose. "See?" She smells the coffee, opens one eye, and regards me warmly.

"You brought me coffee in bed?"

"I did," I say, brushing the hair out of her eyes.

It's been a long time since a girl has made me feel this proud—like I want to show her off to the world and let everyone know she's mine.

"I figured we could spend the day together."

She takes the cup from my hand and sits up against the headboard. "What do you have in mind?"

"First, we're going to drink up this coffee, and then I'm taking you out for some breakfast. Afterwards, we're going to stop by my workshop so you can help me make something."

"Really?" Her eyes brighten.

"Really. Now get your cute ass up and get ready before I change my mind and keep you in this bed all day. Staring at you is really starting to mess with my head."

"Which one?" she asks coyly.

I narrow my eyes in a playful warning, and she quickly moves off the bed. I give her a good smack on the ass and she squeals. Bringing both hands behind my head, I lean back and rest against the headboard, watching her get ready with rapt fascination.

We arrive at my parents' house shortly after eleven. I enter the code on the side of the garage to open up one of the doors. My dad keeps his tools and all of his spare supplies in the garage. He's been letting me store my stuff here to use it as a workspace so I don't have to rent out my own storage unit anymore.

"Whose house is this?" Mia asks, uneasy.

"My parents' house."

"What?!" she shrieks.

I glance over my shoulder to see her panicking. She pulls the sunglasses off her shirt and slides them over her eyes to try and conceal her discomfort, but I've caught on to that trick. Well, I didn't so much catch onto it; more like Eric filled me in, but she doesn't need to know that part. I reach out and grab her waist, bringing her into me. I slide the sunglasses on top of her head and watch her with ease, hoping my relaxed demeanor rubs off.

"Chill, baby."

"I'm not good with parents," she blurts out.

Not wanting her to feel anxious about this, I cup her face in my hands and leisurely part her lips with a slow, passionate kiss to distract her.

It works.

I feel the sensations inside me slowly trickle down and take over. It raises the hair on my arms and the back of my neck—all I can do is let out a deep moan against her lips. Her mouth opens up to me, and I take the opportunity to join our tongues together. She tastes like pumpkin spice and smells like heaven.

I sense her anxiety start to melt away and her body relaxes into mine. I pull back to study her reaction. She looks bewildered, which is exactly what I was shooting for. "Don't worry, both of my parents are working. Besides, even if they were here, don't you think they'd love you as much as I do?" I say earnestly.

Her eyes widen like saucers, and I immediately freeze, processing what I've just said. I'm immobile, still as a statue, while her face is being held in my stiff hands. I'm trying to figure out my next move and what I should say. I think it's safe to assume from the look on her face, that she's doing the same. This isn't how I planned on telling her, but it slipped out. I have no idea how it makes her feel to hear that, but the longer this silence goes on, the more uneasy I feel.

"You love me?" she whispers, in shock.

I let out a heavy sigh and release her face. I run both of my hands through my hair. I'm way out of my element, and I have no idea how to handle this. I feel myself detaching from this conversation to save what little pride I have left, in case that wasn't what she wanted to hear. She looks so confused, either by my admission, or by my reaction.

"Look, let's just forget I said anything and focus on this project I have planned for us, okay?" I say defensively.

"You're shutting me out?" she asks, her voice laced with hurt.

Shit, this is not how I saw this conversation going, and frankly, I'm tired of my ego taking such a substantial hit. Before I can find a way to backpedal out of this mess, she takes me by surprise and steps forward to run her hands up my chest.

"Close your eyes," she orders softly.

I let out an unsure breath, and reluctantly oblige. I sense, rather than feel, her lean in close. She isn't touching me anymore, but I can feel her right there. Not being able to see what she's going to do next puts my body on high alert. Everything is heightened, and my heart is pounding so hard that I can feel it radiating out from my fingertips. I sense her start to move around me, and I mentally follow her, anticipating her whereabouts. She stops behind me and places her hands low on my hips. My body shudders at the sudden contact. She walks me backwards into the garage, guiding me.

The garage is chilly. There's a faint scent of sawdust in the air. I feel the heat from her body envelop me, but all too soon, it's gone. Her feet shuffle across the floor and I can hear her move things around. The garage door starts to close. Suddenly, I feel her in front of me again, and she slides her finger inside the waistband of my jeans, using it to pull me. My eyes are still closed, and I'm being extremely careful not to bump into anything. When she comes to a halt, she gracefully switches our places, so that I'm backed up against what I instantly recognize as my workbench. My hands grip the edge as she deftly unbuckles my belt and kisses my lips.

She's taking the lead on this one. I'll gladly let her dominate me once in a while. I like to see my girl take charge from time to time, but we're not going to make a habit out of this. If she's busy dominating me, who's going to be worshipping her? No one. Can't have that—what a fucking tragedy.

"Is this your way of trying to switch the subject in regard to what I said earlier, because it's working," I half joke, as she removes my belt and lets it fall to the floor.

She goes still for a moment and all I hear is our combined breathing. "No, this is my way of showing you that what you feel for me is reciprocated. I love you, too, Chase," she says with the utmost sincerity.

Well, shit. That did it. That penetrated my heart. I open my eyes so I can see her face when she says that to me a second time. "Say that again, baby."

"I love you," she whispers.

I roughly grab her and crush her lips to mine, effectively destroying her chances at taking the lead. She startles for a moment, but quickly wraps her arms around my neck and kisses me back with painful fervor. She's locked onto me like a life raft during a violent ocean storm. It's like she never wants to let me go, and I feel the exact same way about her.

I hoist her up onto the workbench, and step between her legs to resume kissing. Everything between us is frantic and rushed. I stealthily unzip her hoodie and force it down her shoulders, impatient. Her hands pop open the button on my jeans, and she pulls down the zipper. Halting her progress, I place my hand on her chest and push her backwards until her back is pinned flat against the surface. I grab her legs and use them to move her body, steering her upwards until she's lying lengthwise. I remove my hoodie and lift her head to slide it underneath, ensuring she has something comfortable to rest her head on.

I caress her cheek and stare into her beautiful eyes. There's a ray of light shining through the small window, bringing out the sharpest intensity in them. Around her pupil, there's a solid ring of burning gold, which bleeds out into a pool of forest green. The sight of it steals my breath.

She grabs my wrist, and boldly glides my hand over the tops of her breasts, down her stomach, and into the waistband of her jeans. She places her feet flat on the table, bending her knees. Her legs fold out lazily to the sides as an invitation. I use my other hand to unbutton her pants and slide her zipper down. My fingers skim over the soft fabric of her panties and I can instantly feel how damp she is. I move them to the side and begin to tease her, eliciting a few soft moans. She unabashedly moves against my hand, seeking more pleasure.

I give her body what it needs and slip a finger inside. I add another one and make a "come hither" motion, my fingers brushing up against her wall. She gasps loudly and pushes against my palm to stimulate her clit, and together, the two of us build her up. She lifts her lower back off the table to raise her hips to me, a sign that she wants me to keep at it. I pump her with my fingers and she reaches down between her legs with her other hand to rub her clit. She closes her eyes and absorbs the pleasure. *Fuck.* Watching her do this to herself has got to be the hottest thing I've ever seen. I can't wait to rip these panties off and bury myself deep inside her body where I belong.

"Chase, why are your clothes still on?"

Good question.

I retract my fingers—despite her protest—and taste her passion. Her eyes instantly darken at the visual. I raise my other arm and reach behind my neck to grasp the collar of my shirt and slowly pull it over my head. She eagerly pushes her jeans down, along with her underwear, and drops them to the floor next to my shirt. When she's fully undressed, I pull a condom out from my wallet, and drop my jeans and boxers.

I roll the condom on and boost myself up onto the workbench, crawling over her. Once I'm in place and all lined up, I swiftly sink into her, marveling at how good she feels around me. I begin to move, thoroughly exploring her body, inside and out. I give it to her slow and gentle. She runs her fingers through my hair, giving it a slight pull. I reach down and hitch her leg up on my hip so I can penetrate her more deeply and she groans appreciatively.

Her body tightens up and her legs squeeze my torso. She arches her back and closes her eyes as she's taken into a dramatic climax. I watch her free fall, and my cock throbs as I pump into her two more times before I go rigid, coming hard. My body shudders.

Once the blood returns to the rest of my body, I collapse on top of her and kiss her, lovingly. The garage feels warmer now, and the smell of sex has mixed in the air. I look deeply into her eyes. "I love you."

She gives me another tender kiss before responding with, "I love you, too."

Damn, I couldn't be more taken.

"All right, babe, this is called a surface planer, and all it does is shave off the surface of the wood to make it flat and smooth, which is what we want." I demonstrate how to use it as she watches me closely. We're in the beginning stages of the project, but she has no idea what we're making. I'm going to keep it that way. There's no way we'll finish the majority of this today because she has to go to work, but that's even better. I only want to teach her the basics. She told me she took a shop class in high school, but let's be real, other than guys like me, who actually pays attention in shop?

Once we're finished using the surface planer, I move along and teach her how to build the frames. I set up the dado blade and demonstrate how to line up the stalks properly. I use the small table saw to create a groove in the wood for the long pieces and a tongue in the small pieces, so they can fit together—like a puzzle. I apply some glue onto the joints and connect them while Mia mimics my every move with her frame. I thoroughly double-check her work, and mine—because I'm a perfectionist—and they both look great. We repeat this process until we have a total of five frames done. She's a quick learner, and I must say I never thought watching Mia work with a power saw could be so tempting. *Yeah, that does things to me.*

Due to the noise of the saw, and our intense concentration on the task at hand, it's been relatively quiet between us. I'm double-checking the measurements on some of our work when Mia decides to strike up a conversation.

"Can I ask you something?"

I immediately look up to gauge her reaction. She's not giving anything away. "Of course," I say, unsure of where this is going.

She begins to distract herself by playing with one of the small stalks. "Who's Nicole?"

Big, bright, flashing, warning signs are going off in my head. I set the tape measurer down and give myself a second to decide the best way to respond. Having a conversation about the ex-girlfriend with the current girlfriend can be tricky, and the last thing I'm looking to do is fuck myself in the ass. I want to be forthcoming and honest, but I also don't want to piss her off. I've seen some of my friends, both men and women, get worked up over the smallest things in relationships. I'm hoping Mia's not one of those people because she has no reason to be upset.

I stand up straight, cross my arms over my chest, and casually lean into the workbench, giving her my full attention. "She was my high school girlfriend. We started dating our junior year and the relationship continued when she went off to college."

"Why did you guys break up?"

"She cheated on me during her sophomore year with one of my good friends at the time." I explain matter-of-factly.

Her lips part slightly in surprise. "Jesus, that had to hurt. I'm sorry she did that to you," she mutters.

"Yeah, I was blindsided and heartbroken, to say the least. I never saw that one coming, from either of them, but I'm not sorry she did it. She actually did me a favor in the long run. When you're that young, relationships seem so much more permanent. Then you grow up, gain some perspective, and look back on it, realizing how trivial it all really was."

She tilts her head. "I couldn't agree with you more," she says, smiling.

"What about your past relationships?" I was never going to bring this up, but since she's the one who broached the subject, I decide to take advantage of the opportunity.

"Honestly, there's not much to say. I've had a few flings here and there, but I've never really been in a long-term, committed relationship. I haven't had the time between school, working two jobs, and taking care of my mom. Plus, I had too much baggage at the time. Hell, I still have too much baggage if I'm being completely upfront. I think my longest standing relationship only lasted a couple months—if you can even call it a relationship."

"So, you've never been in love?"

"Not before you, no," she assures with a smirk.

I don't know what it is about that newfound knowledge, but I suddenly feel an overwhelming sense of relief. I know she's not a piece of property, but she's mine. Her heart and body belong to me now, and I intend to keep it that way for as long as she'll let me.

"Did you love Nicole?" she asks quietly, interrupting my borderline-proprietary thoughts.

"At the time, I thought I did. She was my first serious girlfriend, and we were together for years. It wasn't until we broke up and I moved on, that I saw how ordinary our relationship really was. Then when I met you, I felt this strange, exceptional pull that I've never experienced before. Now I know the difference."

"The difference between what?"

"The difference between love and lust. I was comfortable with the relationship, but I was never all in with her, and I think deep down she knew that. Maybe that was one of the things that contributed to her decision to cheat, I don't know." I say, shrugging. "We were both young and content with how things were, but we weren't necessarily happy. She wanted something more, and I wanted more, too. I just didn't know it at the time."

She nods, understanding. "I know what that feels like to be comfortable in your situation because it's routine and it's what you know, but yet you desperately want something more for yourself. You think things like, 'Is this as good as it gets? Is this really what I want for my life?' And I always knew that if you're seriously asking yourself those questions, there's probably something missing."

I unexpectedly reach out and fist my hand in her hair, and draw her to me for a loud, hard kiss. I like that she gets me.

She giggles and turns to kiss the inside of my forearm. She checks the time on her phone. "We better get going. I need to run home and get ready so I can be to work on time."

I let go of her hair and begin to straighten everything up before we leave.

"Are you ever going to tell me what we're building?" she asks, eyes hopeful.

"Nope."

"You know that I'm eventually going to figure out what this is, right? The further we get along on this project, the harder it will be for you to keep it a surprise. I already have a couple guesses as to what it could be."

"You aren't coming back to finish this," I inform her.

"What? Why not?"

"Because this is a special order for someone, and I need to finish it as soon as possible."

"Oh," she says with disappointment etched on her face. It's the same look a kid who was just told "no" by their parents would have. I can't stand that look, so I stroll over and tilt her chin up so she can meet my gaze.

"Babe, I promise to bring you back here, and next time we'll build something together that isn't for an order. You have my word."

This seems to satisfy her, and she gives me a weak smile as a sign of compromise. She takes her safety glasses off and we spend the next few minutes cleaning up together before I have to drive her back home, not wanting to say goodbye.

FIFTEEN

a m e l i a

I finish putting in an order for one of my tables, when I feel my phone vibrate in my apron. It's been going off all evening, but we're so busy that I keep forgetting to run to the back and check it. I hope everything is okay, but the more it vibrates, the more I get a sinking feeling in the pit of my stomach. No one would be calling me this many times if it weren't important. I close my server book and shove it back into the pocket of my apron when I hear my boss call my name.

"Mia, can you please pick up table forty-three for me?" Sherry asks.

Sherry is one of the five managers here at the restaurant, and she's easily my favorite. She's married with two kids, but relatively young, and laid back. She does a good job praising the staff for our efforts, which is always nice to hear—especially when you're new.

It took me a couple weeks, but I'm finally starting to get the hang of things. I'm pulling in quite a bit more money to show for it. Even though I've waitressed before, I was working in a small café and a Swedish diner. Here, these steakhouses are twice the size, and they bring in a lot more business. That makes me feel even better about being on top of my game.

"Absolutely," I respond. I reach for a couple napkins and head over to greet them. After taking their drink order, I double-check my other tables to see if they need anything. I run to the back, grab some glasses, and fill them up accordingly. When I arrive with the drinks in hand, they are ready to order their food. I go around the table, write everything down, and power walk to a computer.

Once their order is placed, one of my customers flags me down to tell me he's ready for his bill, and a table that's not mine asks me for another side of butter. *Ugh, pet peeve.* I let each of them know I'll be right back with that, and head back to the computer to print the gentleman's receipt out. As his bill is printing, Ryan—a fellow server and man-whore extraordinaire—comes up and sets his drinking tray down next to me. Seeing that I'm busy—but not caring because he's Ryan and I have boobs—he decides that now is a good time for some meaningless small talk.

"Hey, Mia, how's it going?" he asks casually, *too* casually.

"Fine," I reply curtly. It's nothing personal, but I don't like needless distractions when I'm working.

"Good. I was actually coming over to see if you'd be interested in going out for a drink together after we get off work?" He moves in a little closer and rests a hip against the counter.

I tear the receipt from the printer and place it in my serving book. Turning to look him in the eye, I prepare to let him down easy.

"I'm sorry, but I can't. I have a boyfriend."

"That doesn't bother me," he says, without batting an eye. "And you shouldn't let it bother you, either. It's not like he'll find out. Besides, I guarantee you'll have more fun with me." He aims to make that sound seductive and enticing, but really, it just comes off creepy.

Great, now he's having delusions of grandeur.

He leans in and my skin crawls.

"Is that so?" a deep voice interjects. "Care to make a wager on that?"

Ryan and I both turn our heads to see a very striking Chase standing with his hands in his front pockets, all calm and collected. His gaze finds mine. Instead of anger being there, like I expect, there's a hint of humor. My heart soars at the fact that he came here to see me, but I'm also wary because I may have a potential pissing contest on my hands.

"Who are you?" Ryan snaps.

"I'm the guy who gets to take Mia home every night. Isn't that right, baby?" He winks at me without missing a beat. "Oh, and for the record—" he looks at the name tag on Ryan's shirt "—Ryan, I keep her fully satisfied. That's why any attempt you make to steal her from me, will be unsuccessful."

Did I mention I'm madly in love with this man? Gotta love a guy who can handle his own and do it using words. Chase is so secure and sure of himself, that he doesn't feel the need to throw a punch to prove something. That's the hottest form of masculinity there is in my book.

I have to bite my lip to contain my smile. Chase's eyes flash with a hint of amusement. I look up at Ryan.

"Well, that about sums it up, don't you think?" Ryan's eyes storm over as he picks up the drinking tray, muttering something about me not being worth his time. He shoves his way past a smirking Chase. So much for letting him down easy.

"What are you doing here?" I ask. Just as he's about to answer, I remember what I have to do. "Hold that thought," I say, and walk off to grab a side of butter and give my table their bill. I deliver both and check on my other table. When it's all good, I swing back around to pick up the serving book with the gentleman's credit card in the top slit and walk over to run it through the computer where Chase is still standing. I swipe the card and my phone buzzes again, reminding me of the second thing I wanted to do earlier. I reach into my pocket, pull it out, and hand it over to Chase.

"This has been going off all night. Can you check my missed calls and find out who's calling me, and why, please? I'm slammed right now."

"Of course." He takes the phone from my hand and unlocks the screen as I get back to tending to the customers.

I'm on a constant rotation with my tables, but finally it seems to be slowing down some. I have no idea where Chase went. I can't find him anywhere so I'm assuming he stepped outside. I grab a to go box from the back and fold it up for one of my tables. When I walk back out, I notice him standing across the restaurant. He beckons me with a casual gesture of his hand. His expression is unreadable.

My heart drops, and I feel myself pale. My throat feels as arid as a desert. I try to swallow to relieve the dryness, but it's no use. I could drink a gallon of water and I still don't think it'd help. I force myself to keep walking towards my table to give them the box. The lady looks up and gives me a "thank you," but all I can manage in return is a tight, artificial smile. I turn back around and make my way towards Chase. I know my limbs are moving, but it feels like there's miles to go before I reach him. The more I walk, the longer that distance seems to stretch. The conversations in the restaurant are all clashing together, making it hard to concentrate.

When I reach him, I let out a slow breath, preparing myself for the worst. "What's wrong?" My throat's so dry it comes out as a rasp.

"That was Hadley. Your mom's in jail and your house got broken into," he says, completely serious.

"What?!" I shriek. "Is she okay?" Tons of scenarios are playing through my head. Everything from my mother being assaulted or harmed in some way, to her beating the shit out of an intruder and catching a battery charge. I don't know which one is more likely at this point. *This cannot be my life.* I look around and notice that we've caught the attention of some customers. Under normal circumstances, I'd be embarrassed, but I'm too shocked to care. Chase grabs my arm and pulls me into a corner near the front of the restaurant.

"Calm down, baby, it could be worse."

"That's easy for you to say," I snap.

"Hey, don't take this out on me. I'm just here to help," he warns.

"Yeah, you and your perfect life are just here to swoop in and save the day, aren't you?" I say venomously. He rears back as if I've slapped him.

"Perfect? You think my life is fucking perfect?"

"Sure seems that way."

"Oh, so is this how it's going to be now?" he asks, motioning between us.

I continue to glare but say nothing. The last thing I need to do is make a scene and lose my job. All I can focus on is how angry I am. I'm mad at my mom for making another mess and going to jail. I'm mad that my house got broken into. I'm mad that I'm stuck here and can't do shit about it. I know it's not fair to take this out on Chase, but he's the easy target.

"You should go home."

"You've got to be kidding—"

"Just go," I say quietly, cutting him off.

He inhales sharply and clenches his jaw. He's pissed. I don't blame him, but I don't have time for coddling. I have to fix yet another one of my mother's messes.

"Don't do this to me, Mia. Don't you dare push me away," he says, shaking his head. He takes a step back, giving himself some space. This is his way of insulating himself from me. I recognize it instantly because I pull the same move all the time with my mom. This must be what she feels like every time she strikes me with her words. I understand it now, sometimes the people we love the hardest in this world, are the ones we end up hurting the most. We feel bad for what we've done, so we keep attacking, trying to make ourselves feel better because we're wounded, too. But when you're in the wrong, there's no one left to protect you but yourself.

I take a moment to try and reason with myself. It's not his fault he had an easier time than I did. That's how it's supposed to be for a child. He had the "normal" upbringing, not me, and it would be foolish to hold that against him. Neither of us can control the cards we were dealt, but we can control how we play them. I can own up to my shit and take full responsibility for my actions. After all, Chase has done nothing but prove that he's here for me through thick and thin.

I keep my gaze fixated on those hard, gorgeous eyes that I adore so much. "I love you, but I need to figure this shit out."

"What are you saying, exactly?" he breathes, clearly nervous. A shadow of fear flickers in his eyes.

"I'm saying that I need to go home and take care of this once and for all." I reach out to touch his cheek, hoping he won't reject me. He looks uncertain, but he doesn't recoil. I run my fingers down the side of his face and along his jaw. His skin is smooth today, and he smells like spice. I bask in his scent one more time for comfort before I have to leave him. I don't really know what I'm going to do, or how long I'm going to be gone. All I know, is I need to talk to my manager and ask for the next few days off so I can try to book a flight out of here tomorrow. I don't want to chance driving in and out of Kansas this time of year.

I take a small step forward and grasp his face in my hands, my thumbs brushing patterns over his cheeks. I lean in to kiss him chastely as an apology, hoping he gets what I'm trying to convey. When I pull back, I notice his eyes have softened, instantly getting the message.

"I'm sorry I snapped."

He lets out the breath he'd been holding, releasing some of the tension from his body.

"You aren't going back there to take care of this by yourself. I'm going with you. Accept that and get over it," he says, making me smile.

"I won't be dealing with this alone. I'll have Hadley. Who knows, we may end up in there right next to my mom. Wouldn't that make for interesting table talk with your family?" I joke.

"You can be my bad girl anytime, but let's keep you out of jail, please. I'm not sure that would go over too well," he says, thawing a little bit.

"Deal," I say. "Now get out of here and go home. I need to talk to my boss and figure out a plan. I'll call you later."

"Fine," he appeases, slipping my phone back into my apron. "But I'm not done having this conversation. If you think I've given up on going back home with you, you're sorely mistaken. I told you once before, I'm persistent." He turns and strolls out the restaurant. I take a moment to gather my thoughts, checking my feelings and family drama at the door.

Time to get back to work.

SIXTEEN

a m e l i a

Sherry was gracious enough to give me the next three days off so I could go back home for a "family emergency." That should be more than enough time to figure all this out and get me back to Austin. I'm grateful to have a job because the cost of my flight was outrageous due to last-minute booking. Chase had to wait on standby for another flight out, but he eventually got one. He was insistent on coming along for support, and once again, he wouldn't take no for an answer.

Shocking, I know.

Hadley is supposed to meet us here at the Salina airport as soon as Chase lands which—according to the arrivals screen—should be any minute. I've already been here for a few hours. I've been wandering around aimlessly, listening to music on my headphones, and reading a book to help pass the time. I think it's safe to say that I'm starting to go stir crazy.

While I was waiting for my connecting flight to board in Dallas, I did some digging and found out my mom was charged with a DUI and disorderly conduct. According to Hadley, she was arrested before the house was broken into, so she's fine. Her bail is set at one thousand dollars, but I'm not going to pay that to get her out. You can go ahead and attribute that to my delayed rage.

Unfortunately, she'll probably be released soon since it's only her first offense. If it were up to me, she'd rot in there. That's quite a change in mentality from a couple months ago. Back then, I would've paid the bail, and taken care of her, no questions asked. Now, I'm only here to assess the house damage, and check to see what all was stolen. If I'm lucky, we won't even have to cross paths. But then again, I'm not exactly known for having luck on my side.

I'm sitting down listening to music, when all of a sudden, a pair of rough hands brush up against my temples and remove my earbuds. I tilt my head back to catch an upside-down glimpse of Mr. Tall, Dark, and Sinful standing behind me. He smiles crookedly and leans down from above to kiss me like the dark angel he is. His halo of brown hair falls around his eyes when our lips touch. My breath catches. *Will it always feel like this?* His kisses are like a powerful sedative coursing through my veins. I instantly feel mollified. No wonder I'm addicted.

He pulls back to drop a tender kiss on my forehead. "Come on, let's get the fuck out of here. I hate airports," he growls.

I text Hadley to let her know that we're both here. Standing up, I grab Raven's Italian leather satchel that she let me use as a carry-on and sling it over my shoulder. Since I'm only going to be here for a couple days, there was no reason to bring a large suitcase. Plus, the majority of my stuff is still in my bedroom at my mom's house. At least, that's what I'm assuming, but I guess we'll see. I don't really care anymore. Whoever it was that broke in, can take the whole damn house. In the long run, they'd probably be doing me a favor.

We turn onto my street and pull into the driveway of my old home. My mom's car is nowhere to be found, but that doesn't surprise me. There's a light dusting of snow on the ground that matches the color of the house. All of the tree branches are cloaked in frost and decorated with icicles. It's beautiful outside at first glance, but it's a deceptive beauty. In reality, everything's completely cold, dead, and lifeless, just like this house sitting in front of us. *How comforting.*

"Ready?" Hadley asks, breaking into my super uplifting thoughts.

"As ready as I'll ever be," I respond, unbuckling my seatbelt.

"Let's get this over with." She turns off the car and unbuckles her seatbelt. Chase opens the rear door and climbs out of the back.

The twenty-minute drive from the airport was nice; I was able to catch up with Hadley. Chase didn't contribute much because he was too busy looking out the window. It occurred to me that he probably doesn't get to see snow very often. I'm sure for him it's a treat, but for me it's a nuisance. When you're a kid, snow is awesome because you get to go sledding in it. When you grow up, it sucks because you have to drive in it.

Hadley and I just finished discussing how her classes have been going at Bethany, and now she's filling me in on all of the town gossip that I've missed.

"Oh, my God, did you hear about that crazy bitch who got arrested last night for a DUI?" she asks, as we're walking up the driveway.

"You know, I think I heard that somewhere, actually. Supposedly, she caught a disorderly conduct charge, too," I play along.

"Yeah, but that doesn't surprise me. Her presence has always been extremely annoying and disruptive, even when she's sleeping. I heard her house got broken into. Talk about karma."

"I know, right? I don't know how that daughter of hers puts up with everything."

"Didn't you hear? Her daughter just up and left. It's long overdue if you ask me, but things are going pretty well for her these days. I always knew she'd land on her feet. She has a new job. Oh, and she met a smoking hot guy. Apparently, he's quite the lover between the sheets."

"Hadley!" I screech and nudge her with my elbow. It knocks her back a couple paces. Chase starts laughing behind us and my hands fly up to cover my flushed cheeks. I'm so thankful it's cold outside because I can attribute the color of my face to the weather. Hadley quickly regains her footing, her long blonde hair bouncing along with each stride. She casually throws an arm around my neck. We make our way up the stairs to the front door. So far, I don't see any evidence that the house was broken into.

I jiggle the doorknob. It's locked. I gave my key to Hadley, just in case there was an emergency and she needed to get into the house. Reading my mind, she reaches into her pocket to pull out her keys. She unlocks the door and pushes it open. I grasp the doorframe and take the first step inside. The wood creaks loudly beneath my feet as a gust of cold air hits me. The temperature inside easily rivals what it feels like outside. I wrap my arms around myself for a sense of warmth and comfort.

It feels like it's been years, rather than months, since I've set foot in here. I'm so far removed from this place now—like I don't belong here anymore. Nothing's changed. It's all exactly as it was. Then it occurs to me why I feel so out of place. It's because one thing *has* changed: me.

The walls are the same horrendous canary color they've always been, but age and smoke residue have dulled the paint over the years. Bottles are scattered on the coffee table and across the floor in disarray. The floorboards are filthy, and there's a stench of stale cigarettes mixed with something else unpleasant that I can't quite pinpoint—s*poiled milk, maybe?*

I flip the light switch to turn on the ceiling fan and air out the room. Nothing happens. Impatiently, I walk until I'm underneath the fan blades and reach up on my tiptoes to yank the chain down. Nada. I try the chain for the light. No dice. I look back at Hadley who looks just as confused as I do.

My God….

The electricity's been shut off.

"Damn it, Mom," I curse under my breath.

Not fully believing it, I stride into the kitchen and turn on the faucet, but nothing comes out. *When did this happen?* I open the fridge and I'm met with a potent sour smell that about knocks me on my ass.

Looks like I've found the mystery stench.

I hold my breath and briskly shut the door. Nothing's frozen in the freezer. To top it off, my mom's vodka stash is missing. In the seven years that I've been dealing with drunk Mom, she's never let her stash deplete—ever. I'm guessing whoever broke in found it and decided to help themselves.

I slam the freezer door out of frustration, making the contents inside shift and rattle. I sulk back into the living room. Chase is standing against the wall with his hands tucked into his coat pockets. He's wearing an uncomfortable expression on his face, and he hasn't spoken a word since we entered the house. It's extremely awkward. I feel humiliated and ashamed that he has to see this. Why couldn't he just stay behind like I'd asked? Does everybody have to be a hero these days?

This is exactly the type of thing I wanted to avoid. No matter how hard he tries, I know he won't be able to *unsee* all of this. I'm afraid he'll treat me differently from here on out. I can't let that happen. My relationship with Chase is the single, most important thing in my world right now, and I don't want that to change. With all of the other uncertainties going on, I need us to remain strong and stable.

"I need to look around and see what's missing," I finally say, breaking the awkward tension in the room. The sooner I finish this, the sooner I can leave. It's a good thing I already made arrangements for Chase and me to stay at Hadley's tonight. Otherwise, we'd be freezing our asses off.

"First, can you show me where they broke in?" I ask Hadley.

She nods and turns to walk past the staircase and down the hallway. I quickly conclude that it has to be the side window in the laundry room. That's the only logical explanation because all of the other windows on the first floor are intact.

Sure enough, the window has been smashed and there's shattered glass all over the floor. I shiver, not because it's cold, but because seeing the window taken out makes this real. Images flash through my head of some creepy man walking through here in the middle of the night with no one to catch him. I'm glad my mom wasn't here when this happened because being all alone in this house would have been traumatizing.

"I would've cleaned up the glass, but I didn't want to touch anything just in case there were fingerprints or something," Hadley explains.

"Prints are shoddy, at best. Temperatures and weather conditions can affect the preservation of fingerprints on surfaces, especially glass. I'm not a cop or anything, but I'm guessing if no one saw this guy break in, then you guys are probably shit-out-of-luck," Chase says. His back is leaned up against the doorway with his foot propped up against the frame. He crosses his arms over his chest.

"How do you know about the fingerprints thing? Are you a CSI junkie that I don't know about? It's okay if you are. Admitting that you have a problem is the very first step to recovery," I tease.

He laughs. "No, I'm a carpenter who spends his days working with wood and glass all day, babe."

"You're a *carpenter*?" Hadley asks in disbelief. She whips her head around. Her brown eyes eagerly find mine. "He's a carpenter?" she whispers. "You told me he was a bartender."

"I'm that, too, but carpentry is my day job," he explains, pushing himself off the doorframe with his foot.

"So hot," she mouths and fans herself.

I swat at her arm. "When are you going to move to Austin? I miss you like crazy."

"After I'm done with college, I'm all yours," she promises with a smile.

"Good, because I really need my other half back.

"Oh, my God. Don't even get me started. It's so boring without you here."

I laugh. "Come on, let's check the house and find out what's missing."

After a quick but seemingly thorough inspection, we find that the only things missing are the alcohol from the freezer, some of my mom's good jewelry, and one of the TVs. Everything else seems to be here. I also discovered the back door was unlocked, so whoever was here, probably used it on their way out. That was an oversight on my part.

I snag a medium-sized cardboard box from my bedroom and head downstairs to tape it over the windowsill in the laundry room. It'll have to do until I can get someone over here to fix it, hopefully tomorrow. Chase is sweeping up all of the broken glass, while Hadley writes down what's missing. We're all quick and efficient, resulting in us being able to get out of here in no time. Thank God for that. We lock up the house behind us, and then we're off to Hadley's place to finally have some fun.

SEVENTEEN

c h a s e

I once read somewhere that the amount of clutter in your house is a direct reflection of how tidy your life and emotions are. Personally, I think that's bullshit. If you ask me, it's all about personality traits. Messy people are messy, and organized people are organized; simple as that. It has nothing to do with the state of your life. But let's consider the possibilities for a minute. If there's even an ounce of truth to that theory, it would certainly help to explain why Nancy's house is as much of a train wreck as she is.

I don't know what I was expecting when I walked in, but what I got was something else entirely. Everything was so dirty and cluttered. There were dishes in the kitchen sink that probably haven't been washed in a month. Stains and cigarette burns covered the upstairs carpet. There were piles of stuff everywhere. I felt claustrophobic. Have you ever seen an episode of *Hoarders?* That's what Nancy's house reminded me of. It looked like something you'd see straight out of that show. I'm supremely confident that jail is a step up for her. At least it's warm in there.

If there's one thing I can take away from this whole experience, it's that I've never appreciated my parents more than I do right now. I almost want to call my mom just to say thank you for putting up with all of my shit and acknowledge all that she and my dad have done. My life wasn't perfect, but at least I grew up in a safe environment where I knew I was loved. Unfortunately, I can't say the same for Mia.

I tried to keep my reaction to a minimum when we did the walkthrough. I could tell Mia was bothered that I saw everything. I'm sure she felt exposed and put on display for all to see, but she'll just have to get over it. I'm not going anywhere. I meant what I said about coming here to support her. I love this girl, and that means I'm here through hell and high water.

When we get to Hadley's place, we order pizza, stay in, and chill. It's too damn cold outside to do anything else. We're all lounging on the couch watching *Shaun of the Dead*. Turns out, Hadley is a zombie fanatic. It's quite entertaining to watch her and Mia go back and forth on what a "real-life" zombie would actually be capable of. I have to give them both props, they know their stuff. These two are fully prepared for an apocalypse at any given moment.

Once the movie is over, it suddenly hits us how tired we all are. I feel like I've been run over by a Mack Truck. All I can think about is my face hitting the cool side of a pillow, and Mia's gorgeous body wrapping around me like a vine. The latter sounds pretty damn good.

"I hope you guys are okay with the futon, because it's either that or the floor," Hadley says.

"The futon is perfect," Mia assures. "Thanks again for picking us up and letting us crash here."

"Yes, thank you, Hadley," I second.

"Anytime. Mia knows that. It sucks that it had to be under these circumstances, but I'm excited regardless." She leaves the room and heads down the hallway.

Hadley is one awesome chick. She's pretty much the blonde version of Mia, so it's no surprise why they get along so well. They share a lot of the same mannerisms, they have similar personalities, and they wear the same styles. Today she's sporting a pair of blue Chucks, skinny jeans, a red tank, and a long-sleeved flannel shirt. She gives off the same hipster vibe that Mia does, although I think Hadley is a little more tomboyish.

She's currently residing in a small, one-bedroom apartment. From the looks of things, it appears she's heavy into art. Her walls are decorated with framed vintage posters and her entertainment center has hand painted designs that run down the sides. The furniture is a bold red, and there are lots of unique, colorful trinkets lying around. The ceiling has occasional water damage spots and the walls have some slight cracks here and there, but it only adds to the energy of her place. Surprisingly, it doesn't look dirty or run down. Contrarily, it's very worn in and eccentric. It all looks effortlessly thrown together, but I can tell she put a lot of thought into the placement of her furniture and decorations.

She reemerges with a thick, heavy blanket in her arms and some spare pillows. She tosses everything down on the futon. "All right, I'm off to bed. You guys help yourselves to whatever. Mia knows her way around, so if you need something, ask her." She looks over at Mia adoringly and says, "'Night, slut," then starts to walk off. She takes a few steps, stops abruptly, and looks back over her shoulder. "By the way, don't even think about tainting my futon. I'll know if you do. I'm everywhere," she warns.

I let out an exasperated sigh. "All right, fine. We'll move it down to the floor."

"Chase!" Mia reproves.

Hadley bursts out laughing. "Don't be so uptight, Mia. I like him already," she says decidedly, and walks out of the room.

Mia's cheeks are crimson, either from embarrassment or anger. Probably both.

"Get over here," I say, tugging her toward me. She stumbles forward a bit and I catch her by the waist. She straightens herself and lets out a heavy breath. I move in to kiss her, but she pulls away. I release my hold on her hips and give her the space she's looking for. She begins to pace back and forth restlessly. Her arms are crossed over her chest as if she's protecting herself from something. I'm trying to read her expression so I can get some idea of what's wrong, but her face is composed. Watching her pace is starting to make me anxious.

"Hey," I say softly. "I'm sorry if I upset you." The only thing that's coming to my mind is the poorly timed joke I made a minute ago.

"No, it's not that. I mean, yes, that was embarrassing, but that's not what's bothering me."

I frown. "Then what's bothering you?"

"Do you really want to know?"

"Lay it on me, babe," I insist.

She wastes no time getting to the point. "I'm worried about what you think of me after seeing the environment I grew up in. I don't want you to think less of me and I don't want to lose you. That puts me in a very compromising position. I went from being solely independent, to depending on you a lot recently. You have the power to take that all away from me. I also feel like I need you. I'm not sure that's a healthy thing. I've never really had anything to compare this to, so I don't know if that's normal or not."

I don't say anything. Instead, I respond by grabbing her face and kissing her deeply, hoping to dispel those silly thoughts from her head. When I pull back to study her reaction, she appears to be even more flustered. It's obviously going to take more than a simple kiss to make her feel better this time. She needs consoling.

"First of all, I love you. Now, let me address the rest of your concerns. If you truly believe I think less of you after today, you are out of your damn mind. If anything, I think more highly of you than I did before—if that's even possible. I got a firsthand glimpse into what your life was like and what you've had to deal with. I don't know how you did it, babe. I find you to be incredibly brave. As for your independence, you are still independent. I know it probably doesn't feel that way all of the time, but you are, I promise. You couldn't be overly dependent on me if you tried, Mia. You don't have that capability in you. One of the perks of being in a relationship is you get to lean on me when you need to, and I you, love. It's all about give and take. I know how important it is for you to be your own person and establish your own life. I would never try to take that away from you. I just want to lessen the burden, that's all.

"And since I'm on a roll, your feelings for me are not unhealthy. I know it's easy for me to say that since I'm the recipient, but it's supposed to feel this way. Love is intense. But I know if I royally fucked up tomorrow, you wouldn't think twice about kicking me to the curb. It would probably hurt like hell, but you'd be able to move on. You wouldn't let the demise of our relationship be the demise of *you*. Don't you see? It takes a strong, healthy person to maintain that. Not everyone can be that stable. Look at what happened to your mom when your dad left. She couldn't deal. And when he died, I think a part of her died right along with him. She may never be able to come back from that." I tilt her chin up. "But you aren't her, baby. You're so much stronger."

She's looking up at me with wide eyes. Her breaths are coming in quick, short pants, like she just finished running a marathon.

I lean forward and press my forehead against hers. "I'm here for you."

Her shoulders relax and she closes her eyes, exhaling a sigh of relief. That's all she needed to hear. She just wanted a little reassurance that I'm not going anywhere.

Her breathing slows to a steady rhythm. We're standing so close that I can feel the swell of her breasts brushing up against my shirt as she inhales. Our heated breaths are lingering on each other's lips and my mouth is so close to touching hers that I can almost taste her. It's excruciating and tantalizing all at once. Thanks to the low-cut black sweater she's wearing, my eyes are met with a wonderful cleavage shot. She has a light dusting of freckles across her chest, and it only adds to her beauty.

Man, she has great tits.

Not a single word passes between us, but we can both sense each other's arousal. She opens her eyes and lets them simmer into mine. I gradually trace her bottom lip with my thumb—so soft and smooth, just like the rest of her body.

"How am I supposed to avoid tainting the futon when you're looking at me like that?" I ask, my tone serious.

"Who said anything about the futon? I had something else in mind," she says with a wicked gleam in her eyes.

Well, damn. Can't argue that. I rest my hands under her jaw and lean in to press my lips into hers, taking my time on the way down. The anticipation is palpable, sweet torture. When our lips finally touch, my heart fails. She feels so good against me. I'll never get tired of it. It's incredible, nothing short of divine.

I free her lips for a moment. "Have I told you how beautiful you look today?"

She shakes her head.

"You look gorgeous," I assure her.

She rolls her eyes. "Shut up and kiss me again."

A genuine smile spreads across my face and we pick right back up where we left off. Her arms snake around my waist and she pulls me in even closer. Our bodies are crushed together with no more room left and it still doesn't feel like we're close enough. I need to be inside her.

Reading my mind, she starts walking me backward without bothering to remove her lips from mine. I'm trying to stay quiet and not trip over anything. I open my eyes to take in my surroundings but hers are still closed. Hadley was right; Mia knows her way around this place like it's her own.

She swings us to the right and moves down a narrow hallway. The first door we pass is closed. I assume that's Hadley's room. The next door is the bathroom. Mia backs me in there, breaks the kiss, and turns on the light. She spins around, gently closes the door, and locks it, barely making a sound. The bathroom is small. The counter is filled with makeup, hair products, and lots of other girl shit. We'll have to work around that. There's no way Hadley is asleep yet, so the goal is to be as quiet as possible. Who am I kidding? She probably already detected us. I don't care.

"Take your pants off," I whisper.

She removes her shoes and begins to undo her jeans. Using both hands, she carefully slides them over her perfect little ass, making an erotic show out of it. My pulse quickens as she shimmies out of them. They drop to the floor in a puddle at her feet. I grasp the hem of my shirt, bringing it up over my head. I throw it off to the side and it makes a faint noise as it hits the floor. I grab her sweater and repeat the process. My eyes roam over every inch her gorgeous figure. Her bra has a front clasp.

Thank you, God.

And while I'm at it, please bless the person who created that.

I take step back and start to unbutton my pants. She grabs ahold of my hands and pushes them out of the way. "No, I want to do that," she whispers firmly. Her fingers deftly undo my jeans and she yanks them down over my thighs, lowering herself down along with them. She adjusts her body so she's perched up on her knees and grabs the waistband of my boxer briefs. Giving it a good tug, my cock springs free, fully ready. She licks her lips in anticipation and looks up at me through a set of long, dark lashes.

She places one hand on my hip and wraps the other one around the base of my cock, easing me into her mouth. Her tongue swirls around the tip and she moans upon her descent, making me quiver. She moves up and down at a steady flow, letting me savor it. She's taking it nice and slow, like I do with her. Unfortunately, tonight won't be one of those slow nights, though. I'm already too wound up.

She eagerly picks up her pace and takes me as far as she can while pumping me with her hand simultaneously. I have to bite my cheek to keep myself quiet because the combination feels so good. Sweet Jesus, this woman can give head. I feel myself building and I know I'm not far from spilling over the edge. If I don't stop this now, I'll finish in her mouth and that's not what I want.

That's a lie.

I do want that—but I want to be inside her more.

I place one hand around her wrist to halt her movements and I bring the other one underneath to cup her chin. She pauses for a moment, then pulls back, releasing my cock from her mouth. She looks up at me with confusion in her eyes.

"You've got me so worked up that I'm about to come in your mouth," I explain. "Get your sexy ass up on that counter. I'll grab the condom out of my wallet."

Relief washes over her. She stands up and moves Hadley's stuff out of the way. I fish my wallet out of my jeans. She turns around to face me and boosts herself up onto the counter. I tear the foil and roll the condom on. I know Hadley is in the next room, and I don't want to disrespect her space, but I can't deny that the risk of getting caught is making this more thrilling. And I'm pretty sure Mia feels the same way since she's the one who initiated it.

"Lean back against the mirror and spread your legs."

She follows my instructions. I step forward to grab her hips and align us. She uses her forearms to prop herself up. Her head rests against the mirror.

I check to make sure she's ready before entering. When I feel how wet she is, I slowly start to sink into her. "Don't. Make. A. Sound," I whisper, as I slide the rest of the way in. Her eyes roll back in bliss. I lazily pull out and thrust into her again. This time a small sound escapes her throat and her head meets the mirror with a thud.

She sits up and repositions herself. She clutches onto the end of the counter while I lift her hips and start to move. She locks her elbows and pushes up off the heels of her hands, giving it back to me. Her legs are bent at the knees and pulled up along my sides. The majority of her weight is being held by me as I give to her again and again.

I reach out and flip both of her bra cups upside-down. The wiring underneath pushes her breasts up in a seductive invitation. I squeeze one in the palm of my hand and use the pad of my thumb to circle her hard nipple. Her head tilts back in pleasure and I move to the other breast and give it the same attention. She begins to pant and noises spill out of her mouth—I love those noises.

But right now, I need her to reel it in so we don't get caught. I cover her mouth with mine in order to muffle the sounds. Tangling my tongue with hers, I continue my movements below the waist. Her breaths are coming faster and faster through her nose. I can tell this is her peak. I start to feel her contract around me, and I explode. My kisses are no longer able to contain her sounds of ecstasy, so I clamp my hand over her mouth until she settles down. It drives me wild that she's so hot for me. If I have my way, she'll always be this uninhibited.

Both our bodies are trembling with aftershocks. I lean in and kiss a path from her breasts up to her neck, worshipping her with my mouth. The intense emotion I have for this woman can't be measured in any way. Love is love. It doesn't matter what form it's in, or whether or not it makes sense to everyone else. It's ours. It's not meant to be analyzed and dissected; it's meant to be experienced.

So what do I do?

I live in the moment and make it last.

"Tell me about your dad," I coax. We're laying down on the futon, face to face, in our pajamas. We spent the last ounce of energy we had satisfying each other's needs and now we're exhausted. I leisurely run my fingers through her hair, knowing how much she likes it. She sighs and scoots in so I can reach the back of her scalp.

"What do you want to know?" she asks.

"What was he like?"

"He was the best. He had this energy about him, I can't really explain it, but people gravitated toward that. He was just an all-around good guy, and a wonderful dad. He was so protective of me, especially in my early teens. He wouldn't let any boys get near me," she says nostalgically. "He was extremely sarcastic, too."

"Just like his daughter," I observe. She smiles and kisses my lips before she continues.

"He was really into old cars and music. He *loved* music. He'd always say that no matter what you're going through in life, there's a song out there that suits your circumstances. Something you can relate to so you don't feel as alone in the world."

"What kind of music did he listen to?"

"Mainly older stuff—records from the sixties and seventies," she explains. "He was kind of a hippy."

"Is that why you listen to so much older music?" I've noticed her song selections on her phone and the various band tees she wears.

"Yes. I've just grown accustomed to it, I guess. What are your parents like?"

"My mom is extremely patient, and very kind. She's had to be in order to raise Meg and me. We pushed her limits growing up—especially me."

"You? A boundary tester? I never would have guessed," she feigns shock.

"Funny coming from you, Miss Independent. You and Hadley—a couple of rebels, living the dream."

"Hey, that's different," she defends. "I didn't have any boundaries to push. My mom didn't care. She only gave a shit about two things: where was her booze, and did I pay the bills on time. So you can't really argue that I was breaking any rules," she says with good humor. I'm glad the mentioning of her mom didn't take this conversation to a darker place.

"Fair enough. As I mentioned before, my mom's a teacher, so she loves children, and learning. She'll read anything and everything she can get her hands on. If she isn't reading, she's watching the home decorating channels for ideas to remodel the house. I'm sure you can imagine how happy that makes my dad, since he and I end up doing most of the work," I say sarcastically. "He's been trying to wean her off that channel for years, but Mom loves her projects, and he can't say no." I shake my head, smirking at the irony. For the first time in my life, I can relate to not being able to say no to a woman.

"What about your dad?"

"My dad and I are a lot alike. We both love to stay busy and are very hard workers. We're pretty family-oriented, too, but that's more my mom's influence. We do family dinner once a week now to keep up with each other, but back when Meg and I were in school, we had family dinners almost every night."

"Weren't you or Meg in any sports? How did that even work?"

"We were," I acknowledge. "Meg was in volleyball and soccer, and I did football and baseball. On the nights we had practice, we would eat late. If we had a game, there wasn't usually a family dinner that night, but my mom always tried. It was important to her, so we made a point to make it important to us."

A slow smile creeps across her face.

"What?" I ask, unable to stop my own smile from forming.

"I'm just picturing you in a baseball uniform. Kinda sexy."

"Is that so? Does that dirty little thought make you oh-so-happy?" I tease. My index finger comes up to tap the end of her nose in a playful manner.

"Immensely so. You know, I'm starting to wonder if you're too good to be true. I don't even think you have any major flaws that I've seen yet. It's really not fair since you've seen all of mine," she pouts.

With a wave of my hand, I proceed to break it down for her. "I assure you, I'm far more flawed than you. You're absolutely perfect in my eyes. I'm just being on my best behavior because I don't want to give you any reason to break up with me," I admit.

Her face falls. "Chase, why would you say that? I'm not going to break up with you. I'm not a hypocrite like that. No one is perfect and I don't expect you to be. Everyone has baggage. I can handle yours." She leans up on her elbow and gives me a serious look. "I'm here for you," she stresses, repeating the same words of comfort that I gave her earlier.

I give her a tight smile and pull her into me. She curls up against my chest, and I wrap my arms around her frame protectively. I get back to running my fingers through her hair until she falls asleep. My mind continues to wander for hours.

EIGHTEEN

a m e l i a

"Get in the car! It's freezing out!" Hadley yells through the window.

"Hold on to your panties! I'm coming!"

We're on our way to my mom's house to meet the guy who's fixing the window. Since Hadley's cupboards were bare this morning, we stopped at the gas station so Chase and I could get some breakfast burritos and cappuccinos.

I hop in the car and unwrap my burrito, hoping food will take my mind off of my nerves. I don't want to go back into that house again, but I know I have to. After a few bites, I take a sip of my coffee to help warm me up. It burns my tongue immediately. Rookie mistake for a coffee drinker, but my mind is too preoccupied. *Damn, I won't be able to taste the burrito now.* I stick out my bottom lip, pouting like a petulant child.

When we turn onto my street, I see my mom's car in the driveway. I knew she'd be out of there by now. I haven't talked to her since I hung up on our last conversation. I don't even know what to say at this point. I take a few moments to mentally prepare myself before I have to get out of the car. Something's different. Is it Chase being here? Probably, but I trust him.

I swallow past the knot in my throat and open the car door. We're supposed to be meeting the window guy here in ten minutes, so we're a little early. After we left last night, I called the utility company and paid a good portion of my mom's bill to get the power turned back on. They said it could take up to twenty-four hours, so we may very well be walking into a dim, cold house again.

Hypercautious, I walk up the porch steps. My legs feel like they have weights strapped to them. It's taking every ounce of strength I have to keep moving forward. When I approach the door, a feeling of dread flows through me. It's unlocked. I make myself open it and take a step inside.

"Hello?" I call out, anxiously awaiting an answer. A few seconds go by, but there's no response.

"Mom?"

Silence.

She must be passed out drunk. I'm sure after spending a night in jail, which would have sobered her up, she couldn't wait to hit the bottle again. I reluctantly walk farther inside as Chase and Hadley follow. I notice a pack of cigarettes sitting on the coffee table in the living room. Those weren't there last night. My mom isn't on the couch, so I'm assuming she's still in bed. I gingerly walk upstairs. It's so cold—both inside and outside—but I'm sweating underneath my coat.

I manage the few steps down the hallway without too much inner drama and plant my feet in front of my mom's bedroom door. I give two quick courtesy rasps and anxiously peer inside. She's not on the bed. I push my way in past all the clutter on the ground and look around. *Where is she?*

I head back out into the hallway. Chase and Hadley are standing at the bottom of the stairs talking to each other.

"I'm going to get a few things out of my room real quick."

"Sounds good, baby," Chase responds. I'm glad he isn't as uncomfortable as he was last night.

I maneuver around all the junk in the hallway and clutch my doorframe to hold myself steady. I carefully leap into my bedroom, jumping over a pile of her laundry. Looking up from the floor, I come to an abrupt halt when I see my mom lying down on my bed.

My heart plummets.

She's lying on her side, staring up at me. Only, she's not. She's off somewhere in the distance. Her face is an ashy gray, and her eyes are frozen wide open with dark hues shadowing underneath. I stare at her, bewildered, and completely unable to move. I feel like I've just had the wind knocked out of me. I know what I'm looking at, but I'm not *seeing* it—I'm not processing it. My mind's not letting me.

I can't move.

I can't breathe.

I think I'm in some kind of shock, but I can't bring myself to look away. I know that once I look away and break the trance, this will all become real. I won't be able to *not* process it anymore, and I'm not ready for that. So I just stand here and stare, dumbfounded and numb. I don't care if I have to stand in this very spot for the rest of eternity. I'm not moving.

I'm not.

Only, I am.

My legs begin to sway as a broken sob escapes my throat. "Mom?" I whisper. A lone tear rolls down my cheek. "Mom, please wake up."

The room starts to spin—not like a drunk spin—but a chaotic, my-entire-world-has-just-been-flipped-upside-down, spin. A wave of nausea and grief roils my stomach. I try to swallow the bile down, but I can't fight it. I bend over and grasp my knees for support as I vomit. Coughing and panting, my stomach muscles lock up again. My chest heaves as another mouthful comes up and spills out. I wipe the sweat from my forehead using the back of my arm.

"This isn't happening to me. Not again," I whisper to myself, shaking my head in denial.

I take a deep breath and boldly look back up. Her eyes are as cold and lifeless as the rest of her body. When my mind finally allows me to look at something else other than her or the floor, I notice an empty bottle of prescription pills tipped over on the nightstand. *She doesn't have any prescriptions…*

I feel sick again.

Oh, God…she killed herself.

"No," I sob. "No, no, no!"

Somewhere far off, I hear the sound of footsteps rushing up the stairs. "Mia, what's wrong?!" Chase yells, panicked.

I can't form an answer through the tears. Hadley and Chase bump into each other as they both try to get through the doorway.

"Oh, my God," Hadley gasps in horror. She tries to walk into the room, but Chase holds out his arm to prevent her from stepping in my vomit. She looks down in confusion, then it all registers. I know how disgusting this must look, but I'm so glad she doesn't say anything about it.

Chase's hands wrap around my torso. He pulls me up and spins me around to face him. His hands come up to grip my face. "We need to get you out of here," he says slowly, as if he were talking to a child.

"This is all my fault," I say inconsolably.

"Mia, look at me," he commands.

I can hardly see him through all the tears, so I zone out. Anything is better than being trapped in this moment. It's like I'm stuck in a freeze frame. I'd give anything to be able to press rewind or fast forward.

"Mia!" He shakes me, trying to get me to snap out of it.

My eyes find his. He uses the pads of his thumbs to try and brush my tears away, but they keep coming. It's a never-ending flow of heartache.

"This is not your fault. Do you understand? This is not your fault," he repeats.

I don't answer him. I can't. I have absolutely nothing left to give.

"Hadley?" She doesn't answer him either. "Hadley!" he calls out. Her gaze snaps up from my mother's body.

"I need you to keep it together for a little while longer and take Mia downstairs, okay?" he asks.

She nods, but it comes off more routine than response. It's like she's saying yes, but she doesn't know what she's saying yes to. She's just as out of it as I am.

Realizing this, Chase grabs my upper arm and brings his other hand around my lower back. He walks me out into the hall and back down the stairs. I can't feel my body anymore. I know I'm walking, but it feels like someone else is doing all the movements. Once we reach the living room, he gently sits me down on the couch. He crouches down in front of me and looks up, his hands covering mine.

"I'll be right back, baby. I love you. Whatever you need, I'm here for you. Let me take care of this," he pleads.

"The window guy," I whisper. I don't know what makes me think of that, but I don't want him in the house.

"Shit," Chase mutters. He runs both hands through his hair. "I'll deal with it. Just stay here, okay?"

I barely manage a nod. He gives me a swift kiss on my forehead and heads back upstairs. I'm left sitting alone on the couch, trying to block out the images of what I just saw. I've been through more in twenty-two years than most people have been through in fifty. My struggles have made me resilient, but I'm not so sure I can bounce back from this one. At the end of the day, there's only so much one person can take, and I'm pretty sure I've reached my limit.

NINETEEN

c h a s e

After Mia found her mom's body, she went into total reclusion. I haven't heard from her since we got back to Austin—that was six days ago. The entire flight back was nothing but stark silence between us. I've called her multiple times and left countless voicemails, but she won't respond. I ended up calling Raven just to find out how she's holding up. Raven said she hardly ever comes out of her room, and she hasn't been eating much. That concerns me. I know she's depressed, but I don't want her slipping further and further down into the abyss. She needs to be able to come out of this stronger on the other side. I *need* her to be able to come back from this, because the thought of losing her in any way completely shreds me.

I've thought about going over there and showing up announced, but Raven talks me out of it every time. She thinks I need to give Mia the space she deserves. I'm trying to respect that, but it's hard. What if she needs me and I'm not there? I feel like I don't even know what to do anymore. I'm clueless when it comes to dealing with stuff like this. I'm lucky enough to still have all of my close family members and friends around.

Feeling useless and defeated over the situation, I decide to head to Meg's house to help me get my mind off Mia for a while. I have some time to kill before I have to work tonight, and I don't want to spend it moping around my apartment and beating myself up for shit that's out of my control. I throw on my leather jacket and grab my keys in a hurry. I can't get out of here soon enough.

"What do you *mean* you're going to see how it plays out?" Meg raises her voice. She swivels around in her chair and shoots me a stern look over the rim of her reading glasses. She's working from home today. We are in her office arguing about my next move with Mia. So much for taking her off my mind, not that I could ever do that anyway. She's been consuming my thoughts since the moment I met her.

"There's nothing I can do, Meg. I've tried talking to her, calling her, texting her—everything short of fucking telegramming her. She won't respond."

"Of course she won't, she's grieving. She probably doesn't want to talk about it. That doesn't mean you just throw in the towel and call it quits," she says that like it's the most obvious thing in the world.

"I'm not calling it quits, but I don't know what more I can do."

"Oh, that's such a cop-out, and you know it. Fight for her, Chase. In all my life I've never known you to take no for an answer, so what's changed?"

"I fell in love and put someone else's needs above my own! That's what fucking changed!" I yell and slam my fist against the plush sofa.

Meg jumps back slightly, surprised at my outburst. I'm trying to find some way to expel all of my frustration, but nothing helps. The only person who can make me feel better is Mia.

The room falls into a deafening silence. I stand up and pace back and forth in angry strides, with Meg watching me intently. She has one leg crossed over the other. Her shoe is tapping against the floor impatiently. Her arms are folded over her chest, and she's giving me her classic "check yourself" look. I take few deep breaths and try to reel in my anger. I'm frustrated that she's right. When have I ever let someone get in the way of something I want? Although in this case, the one I want is the very same person who's standing in my way.

"I'm walking a fine line here, Meg. I'm trying to respect her space like she asked me to, and be a good boyfriend at the same time," I explain a little more calmly.

"I understand that, but she needs you. Just because she may not want to talk about it, doesn't mean she doesn't want you there. She may say she wants to be left alone, but I'm willing to bet that's not the case. I think now, more than ever, she needs your support. She's probably just too proud to ask for it, especially if she's used to taking care of herself like you say she is. We women don't want to ask for things that we feel should be no-brainers to our men."

"Well then, what do you suggest I do, Dr. Phil?" I ask sarcastically.

"You tell me," she challenges. "You know her better than almost anyone, so you should know exactly what she needs. Figure it out." She leisurely spins her chair back around and resumes working on her laptop.

"Unbelievable. Why can't you women just tell us what you want?" I ask, frustrated.

"Why can't men take a hint?" she retorts.

"Whatever, I'm out of here," I say, heading for the door.

"Chase?" she calls over her shoulder.

I stop and take a deep breath, then look over at her.

"I got you," she says warmly.

That's what I always say to her when she's upset. It's my way of telling her I love her. We stare at each other for a minute or two, before I crack a slight smile. It's the first one I've been able to manage since we found Mia's mom.

"Right back at you, Meg."

"If it's meant to be, it will all work out," she assures me.

Fuck that mentality. Fate may have brought her to me, but it certainly won't be what keeps the relationship together. Undeniable love, communication, and mind-blowing sex will make it last—in that order. After all, everyone knows that anything worth having is worth fighting for, and Mia is definitely worth having.

• • •

"Hey, what's up, man?" Eric asks, when I walk into his apartment. He's sitting on the couch playing *Call of Duty* with his eyes glued to the TV screen. I walk into the kitchen and grab a beer out of the fridge, even though it's only four o'clock in the afternoon. I figure after the shitty week I've had, I'm entitled to it—sue me. I twist the cap off and walk over to take a seat next to him.

"Not much. Just been working and trying to get ahold of Mia."

At the mentioning of Mia's name, he pauses the game and sets his controller down on the couch. "I was going to ask you how she was holding up. I was over there a few days ago, but she wouldn't come out of her room. I tried breaking down her door to get her to talk to me, but it got me nowhere."

"That seems to be a theme with her lately. Hell, you probably know more than I do at this point. She hasn't bothered to talk to me since we got back."

"Naw, man, I only know what Raven tells me, which isn't much. I don't even think she knows what's going on either."

I set my beer down on the end table and lean forward. "I'm really trying to be supportive and understanding, but between you and me, I'm running out of patience. I can respect that she wanted the first couple days to herself, but to not even acknowledge that I've been basically stalking her—that pisses me off." A pang of guilt twists in my chest as those words leave my mouth. I feel like the world's shittiest boyfriend. My girlfriend loses her mom, and I get pissy because she won't talk to me. How mature am I? "I feel like a bad guy for saying that," I admit aloud. I fall back into the couch and rest my hands on my thighs.

"I don't think that makes you a bad guy. It's a fucked-up situation all the way around. Shit, if it were me, I'd be just as frustrated as you are. I think for her to deliberately ignore all of us is selfish. I know she's mourning the loss of her mom, but at least let us know you are...well...for lack of a better term—okay. She has people who care about her that she can lean on. If she's not going to utilize that, she should at least acknowledge it," he says irritably.

I reach over and take a few more sips of my beer and wonder what Mia is doing at this very moment. *Is she okay? Has she come out of her room? Is she in bed crying? Is she drinking herself into a coma? Is Raven there with her?*

I rest my beer between my knees and rub my eyes, exhausted. I can't keep doing this to myself. I'm all fucked up because of her. When shit's not right with her, shit's not right with me. I can't concentrate on anything because all I'm doing is thinking about what I could do or say to make this better, but I come up short every time. I'm a fixer, dammit. So why can't I fix this?

TWENTY

a m e l i a

I used to believe that it was always my dad and me against the world. Then, when he died, it was only me against the world. I'd never felt so alone before. Sure, I had friends, but there was no one left to take care of me and make me feel safe anymore. Looking back now, I realize how naïve I was. The notion that I was alone is laughable. I had no idea what being alone truly felt like—until now.

It's been a week and a half since my mom died, and all I can think about is what would've happened if I arrived at the house ten minutes earlier? Would she have still been alive? Could I have saved her? I went to bed the night before, knowing she was alive, and by morning she was dead. In the blink of an eye, I became an orphan. I still can't quite wrap my head around that. I didn't even get to say a proper goodbye. The last words she ever heard to come out of my mouth were empty threats and vicious insults.

The irony of the whole thing is that I was so worried to move down here in the first place because I didn't want something to happen to her while I was gone. But she ended up dying while I was less than five minutes away. I don't know if that makes me feel better, or worse. I still feel like it's all my fault. Maybe if I never would have left, she never would have done that to herself? I don't know. I don't know anything anymore.

Instead of giving her a proper burial, I went with cremation. There wasn't enough money left over to take care of a casket, a headstone, a burial lot, and funeral costs. Besides, the only people that would've showed up to her funeral would've been Hadley, Chase, and me. She had no family nearby, and she had alienated all of her friends years ago. I wouldn't know how to get in touch with any of those people even if I tried.

I called the bank and told them there was no way I could pay all of her back payments in order to keep the house, so they are taking it. Hadley and Chase helped me move most of the furniture and my belongings into a storage unit. I left the rest behind. I have no home to go back to anymore. If I can't make it work here with Raven, I'll be homeless. Orphaned and homeless—how's that for a combination? As much as I never wanted to go back, it was comforting to have the option in the back of my mind, just in case.

Tired of feeling hopeless and dead inside, I throw the covers back and slowly roll out of bed. I walk over to my window and open my blinds for the first time since I got back. The gloomy weather outside completely reflects my current mood. It's light out, but thankfully, the sun is nowhere to be found.

Grabbing one of my last clean outfits off the floor, I head to the bathroom for my first shower in three days. Believe me, this is an improvement from last week. Everything took a major hit when my mom died. Finances, hygiene, appetite, mental health, physical health, relationships with friends, Chase...*Chase*. Just thinking about him hurts. He's been calling and texting me nonstop since we got back. I've been ignoring everyone to make it all go away. Instead of fixing it like I should, I'm running to avoid feeling any more guilt.

I open the door and trudge down the hall towards the bathroom. Raven has finals this week, so she hasn't been home much. She rarely left the apartment last week. She wanted to be near me in case I needed any support, but other than to pee and force myself to eat a little food, I didn't leave my room. The first night I got back, she hugged me while I sobbed on the couch, but I've been isolating myself ever since.

I walk into the bathroom, toss my clothes onto the floor, and lean over to turn on the shower. Water spurts out from the showerhead and hits my upper arm, making me shiver. Realizing that I forgot a towel, I head back to my room. When I walk in I notice my phone flashing on my nightstand. I pick it up.

Chase: *Are you ever going to talk to me again? I miss you.*

A spasm assaults my chest when I read his message. I scroll through all of the other previous texts he has sent me within the last ten days, and my guilt comes back tenfold. I open up a new message to say something back, but as always, I got nothing. I press the back button and set my phone down. I'll deal with that later. First, I have to shower and get ready for my first day back at work. My bosses were more than accommodating to give me time off, but now it's time to start living again.

One day at a time.

No...scratch that.

One hour at a time.

• • •

Work sucked.

It was difficult to focus when everyone kept asking me questions. *"Are you okay, Mia?" "How are you holding up?"* Then there's my favorite comment: *"I'm so sorry for your loss."*

No, they aren't. They never even met my mother and they barely know me. I know it's common courtesy, and they're just trying to be nice, but that's exactly my point. Those things are only said out of courtesy. It's not from the heart. If you don't mean it, then don't say it. Simple as that.

When I walk into the apartment, I'm met with a deafening silence. I hate silence when I'm grieving. All it does is make me think about everything that I don't want to remember. I think about my mom, and what her dead body looked like when she was lying on my bed staring up at me, her eyes vacant. I think about the empty bottle of pills on the nightstand beside her. I think about what an awful daughter I was those last few years. All of the horrible things I said to her, I'd take them back in a heartbeat. Instead of giving her grief, I should've given her hugs. Instead of saying she was a worthless mom, I should've said "I love you." Instead of leaving her behind, I should've stayed.

Flashbacks from my childhood begin to play through my head like an old movie reel. Happy ones—where she, my dad, and I were a family. Memories where we were at the park for a family picnic and she would push me on the swings as high as I could go. Memories where she held me tight and told me how much she loved me before she tucked me in at night. I remember the delicious smell of hot chocolate in the wintertime. When my dad and I got home from sledding, she'd have two steaming cups waiting for us. She'd always put marshmallows in mine because she knew how much I loved that. Then my dad would try to steal them out of my cup when she wasn't looking, only to end up pulling out the bag and giving me double the amount I initially had. It's the simple things, you know? Those are what I miss the most.

Looking back, I realize what an amazing mom she really was. She had more than her fair share of flaws, but I do believe, deep down, she loved me...even at her worst. I'd like to think that she always loved my dad, even after they split, and that's why she could never get her life together—because she just couldn't bear to live without him. I hope they are both happy somewhere together and madly in love like they used to be. In all those years, neither one of them ever remarried—I'd like to think there's a reason for that.

Thinking about my parents when they were at their best soothes my soul and brings me a sliver of inner peace. It's not much, but it's something. It's a beacon of light during a dark and tumultuous time, and I'll gladly take it.

I remove my shoes and head to my bedroom so I can change out of my uniform, crawl into bed, and collapse. I've done my big thing for the day, and there's nothing left to give. Not to get all "poor me" about this, but I think I deserve a pat on the back for getting out of the apartment. When I open my bedroom door, my eyes collide with another set—these ones are blue. I let out a scream and jump back in surprise. My hand flies up to my chest to steady my heart.

"Easy there."

"Jesus, Eric. What the hell are you doing here?"

"Come, come," he pats a seat on the bed next to him.

"What's this about?" For some reason, I feel like I'm walking into the principal's office.

"I think you already know what this is about."

Could he be any more melodramatic?

I pull my phone out of my pocket and toss it onto the bed. I remove my apron and nametag. Eric picks the phone up and waves it in front of me.

"Well, well, lookie here," he says casually, sarcastically. "So you *do* have a phone."

I roll my eyes and strut over to the bed. I take a seat next to him, and relish in how good it feels to be off my feet after an eight-hour shift. I make a move to steal my phone back, but he extends his arm out to the side, holding it out of my reach.

"Give it back, Eric," I snap.

"No," he says defiantly. "Not until you give me a good reason as to why you're ignoring me."

"What are you talking about?" I feign ignorance.

"Don't play dumb with me, Mia. Leave that to the real stupid chicks out there because there're plenty of them to go around."

"You would know," I accuse.

He narrows his eyes and his lips pull into a thin line. "I'm going to assume you aren't referring to your best friend when you say that."

"Of course I'm not!" I defend, insulted. Feeling irritated with his close proximity, I stand up and move over by the door. "Once again, Eric, what do you want?" I'm impatient and I was over this conversation before it even started.

"I told you what I want, now answer me. Why have you been hiding out and ignoring everyone?"

"What do you want me to say? You want me to say I'm sorry? You want me to tell you that I'm A-Okay? Is that what you want to hear?"

"I don't give a damn if we sit here and talk about the fucking weather, but for the love of God, say something!" he shouts.

"Fuck you!" I shout back and give him the finger to boot. It feels good to yell. I've been bottled up for days. "You're such an asshole! I didn't ask you to waltz in here and invade my personal space. Quit trying to get me to talk about it. I'll talk about it when I'm damn well ready to," I say, resentful.

He shakes his head back and forth. "Nope, that doesn't work for me. I've given you plenty of space and time, and I'm not leaving until you talk."

"Yes, you are," I guarantee, extending my arm and pointing towards the door, letting him know it's time for him to go.

"Fuck that. You've shut me out long enough. I'm not letting you kick me out of here just because you'd rather bury your head in the sand instead of facing how you really feel."

"You've got to be joking?" I ask, floored.

"Nope, I'm serious. *Dead* serious...no pun intended," he says, expressionless.

We stare at each other for a long moment, neither one of us willing to back down. We take turns blinking, somewhat mystified. When we can't hold it in any longer, we both burst out laughing. It starts out as a fit of giggles and quickly escalates into full-on guffaws. It's wonderful, cathartic laughter. Eric folds over onto his side and grips his stomach, trying to control himself. I back up against the wall and slide down to the floor with tears in my eyes.

We laugh until our stomachs hurt and I feel the urge to piss my pants. Once we've calmed down, I look up to find him lying on his back, staring at my ceiling. He tilts his head in my direction and gives me one of the most endearing smiles that I've ever seen. It would make any woman swoon. He rolls off the bed and crawls down onto the floor by my side. Bringing his arm up over my head, he settles it around my shoulders. I lean my head against his chest and just let him hold me for a minute before we speak.

"In the strangest way, I knew it was coming." I whisper softly. "I mean, I was shocked to walk into my room and find her like that, but somewhere deep down in my gut, I knew something wasn't right. I felt it before I even walked in the house."

"Was there a funeral service?"

I shake my head. "There wasn't enough money."

"What about Chase?"

"What about him?" I don't want to acknowledge how I really feel about all that.

"Have y'all talked?"

"No. He's been trying to get a hold of me, but I haven't responded," I say, feeling guilty.

"You should do that. He loves you, you know. He came over to my place last week to talk about everything. You've really got him by the balls. The guy just isn't right without you. Take it from me, locking down a guy like Chase is hard to do. It takes a pretty special woman to make him want to forfeit everything for a chance to be with you. I know he'll treat you right, but you gotta treat him right, too. And this whole ignoring him thing—that isn't right, and you know it."

I felt guilty before, but now I feel absolutely horrible. I was so concerned early on about whether or not he'd hurt me, it never crossed my mind that I might be the one to end up hurting him. From the moment he sat down on Eric's couch and annoyed the hell out of me, Chase has given me nothing short of everything he has. He's never held anything back and he's made me far happier than I ever thought I could be.

"Are you going to be okay?" Eric asks after a long moment.

I let out a deep breath. "I think so. At first, I thought I'd never survive it, but it's slowly becoming a little more bearable. I have my ups and downs."

"Why didn't you come to us for support? You know we would've been there for you—that we *have* been here for you."

"I know but I couldn't, Eric. I couldn't even function. I'm dealing the only way I know how," I explain.

"Well, your version of dealing with life-changing issues completely blows," he teases. "We're going to have to work on that. Fortunately for you, I think you're about out of those, because short of losing a friend, you've got no one left to lose. Welcome to the club," he half jokes. I know he's trying to lighten the mood, but he can't mask the pain and regret in his voice when he says that.

He's right; I don't have much left to lose. I've lost my mom, my dad, my house, my sanity, and possibly my boyfriend. I've sacrificed everything. I dropped out of school, gave up my life, and took on the stress of taking care of my mom—just to have her commit suicide in the end. It was all for nothing. I wasted years of my life that I'll never get back, and for what? To watch it all come crashing down? The thought makes me giggle. It's not supposed to be funny, but it is. Sometimes things get so awful in life, all you can do is laugh.

I tilt my head up to catch a glimpse of Eric's handsome face. "Thank you, Eric. Thank you for everything," I say sincerely. He's done more for me in ten minutes than I've done for myself in ten days.

"No problem, Strawberry. I don't know about you, but I think it's time to come out of hiding, don't you agree?" He looks down at me and smiles.

"Yeah, yeah, whatever," I mutter petulantly.

He laughs and pulls his knees up to his chest. He stands up, turns to face me, and offers his hand. I reach up and take it. His fingers curl around mine and he pulls me up. He's done that in more ways than one tonight.

As I'm walking him to the front door, he turns to me and says, "I know it's not even Christmas yet, but don't make any plans for New Year's Eve, okay?"

"Why, what's going on?"

"I'm having another party and your appearance is mandatory. You owe me that after what you've put me through these last couple weeks."

"What I've put you through? What about what I've had to go through?"

"Whatever. There you go, making it all about you again," he feigns annoyance. He opens the door and pulls me into a tight hug. He lays a kiss on top of my head and pulls away. "Tell Raven I'm coming for her later after she gets off work."

"Will do," I assure him.

"Later, Strawberry," he grins and closes the door on his way out.

When the door shuts, I'm left with another round of silence. Only this time, I don't feel quite so alone.

TWENTY-ONE

chase

If you're wondering what's been helping me get by lately, the answer is work. Since Christmas is right around the corner, I'm far busier than usual—and I'm a pretty busy guy to begin with. But instead of being all in like I normally am, I've been going through the motions. We have a large order for a dining set, so, Jim (my dad's longtime friend and co-worker) and I have been focusing on that today. He knew right away that something was off, but instead of grilling me about it, he just kept to himself. That's one of the many reasons why I enjoy working with him.

I've never made a habit of bringing my personal problems to work, but it's taken more than I'd like to admit for me to keep my mind off Mia. I still haven't heard from her, and I've given up on trying. I don't even know where we stand anymore. I'm preparing one final gesture to get her to come around, and if I don't hear from her, I'm throwing in the towel. This is the last-ditch effort. There's only so much I can do. I can't make her want this relationship as much as I do, and I can't force her to talk to me when she clearly isn't ready.

I've just finished staining some dining chairs when I feel my phone vibrate in my pocket. I take my gloves off and fish it out of my jeans. I eagerly check the screen, desperately hoping to see Mia's name. No such luck. I swipe my finger across and answer the call.

"Hey, Christa," I greet.

"Hey, stranger. How have you been?" she asks, cheerful.

"Pretty good," I lie. "Just been busy working. What about you?"

"Oh, same old. Rachel is finally moving out, so I'm on the hunt for a new roommate. It's long overdue, that bitch's departure. I'm going to do some shopping today to celebrate," she says giddily.

"You're terrible." I don't even try to sound like I'm joking when I say that. She's never gotten along with Rachel, but then again, Christa has trouble getting along with most women.

"I know I am," she says. "So, how are you and Mia doing?" There's no hostility in her voice when she asks that, just pure curiosity.

"We've been better," I admit. "Mia lost her mom a couple weeks ago and it's been putting some strain on our relationship."

"Oh, no, what happened?"

"We don't really know yet," I lie again. I'm not sure if Mia wants people knowing what Nancy's cause of death was. And since her and Christa didn't get off to the best start, I don't want to share that information without her consent. We may not be talking at the moment, but I still love the girl more than anything, and I want to respect her privacy.

"That's too bad. I hope you guys can work it out. Please tell her I'm sorry for her loss," she says sincerely.

"Thank you, Christa. I will."

If only I could….

"Well, the real reason why I'm calling is to check and see if you're going to Eric's New Year's Eve party."

"Yeah, I'm planning on it," I say cautiously.

"Me too. I think it will be good for both of us to see each other again and talk some things out. I miss you."

A feeling of unease travels through me. I'm not sure Mia would be on board with Christa and I spending time together at the party, but what can I do? It's not like I can just call up my own girlfriend and talk to her about it. And I can't tell Christa not to go to the party because Eric obviously invited her. I could stay home and not go myself, but I'm not going to do that. I need the distraction right now.

"I guess I'll see you there then," I say, slightly uncomfortable. "But hey, I really need to get back to work," I say, cutting the conversation short.

"Sounds good," she says. "I'll talk to you later then."

"Yep, talk to you later." I press my thumb on the screen to end the call and slide my phone back into my pocket.

I know I'm not doing anything inappropriate, but this feels wrong. I feel like I'm going behind Mia's back. The thought makes me feel uneasy. I don't spend too much time dwelling on it, though.

If she has an issue, she can pick up the damn phone and call me back for once.

After staying late to catch up on orders, I call it a day and head to my parents' house. I need to finish up the project I've been working on in the garage. I cruise up the driveway and put the car in park. I called my mom ahead of time and told her I was coming, so she already has the garage door open.

Walking in, I flip on the light switch and set my keys down on my workbench. Each time I come in here and see that, I'm reminded of Mia's naked body draped across it, aroused and waiting for me. The thought instantly makes me hard. It's been a while. I can't help it when my thoughts drift to the way her eyes darken when I boss her around in the bedroom. She likes that, but only in the bedroom.

I miss her so much. I miss the smell of strawberries and vanilla in her hair. I miss the way she builds up my ego, then two seconds later, she turns around and shatters it. I miss holding her and making her smile. I miss hearing her sing really bad eighties music in the shower, while I'm getting ready in the morning. But most of all, I miss the way she makes me feel when I'm around her. Like I'm the only person that matters. To everyone else, she may be a stranger— someone you pass by on the sidewalk or in the store, but to me, she's everything.

A light knock on the door breaks me from my thoughts. I turn around to see my mom, a concerned look on her face. She steps forward with a warm plate of food in her hands.

"I made supper earlier. I thought you might like some leftovers while you work out here," she says warmly.

I reach out and take the plate. "Thanks, Mom," I say, forcing a smile.

She steps farther into the garage and walks over to my father's workbench. Her fingers glide over the surface, picking up some sawdust along the way. "You know, every time your father and I would have an argument, he'd come out here and work on something to help take his mind off it. Sometimes he'd be out in this garage for hours, building away until he was ready to talk about it."

"I remember that. There were times I used to be out here helping him," I remind her.

"I know," she smiles fondly. "He's always so stubborn—just like you."

I break eye contact and set the plate down. "Where are you going with this one, Mom?"

"Whatever's going on between you and Mia, it will eventually pass."

"I'm not so sure about that. I haven't heard from her in weeks."

"Do you love her?"

Her question hits me like a ton of bricks. I grip my workbench and drop my head. Closing my eyes, I take a deep breath and exhale.

"We don't have to talk about it if you don't want to," she assures me.

"Without question," I say, opening my eyes again. I straighten up and glance at her, my expression serious. "I'm sure you're thinking that's highly unlikely since we haven't been together for very long, but I'm telling you, I'm crazy in love with her."

"I'm not surprised," she responds, unfazed.

"You're not going to stand here and tell me it's too soon?" I ask, not understanding her reaction. My mom has never been the type of woman who throws caution to the wind. She's very practical and careful with her choices. She dated my dad for seven years before she married him. In her mind, that's a shotgun wedding.

"Don't look so surprised," she says, her voice filled with humor.

"I'm sorry. I guess I was expecting a big lecture from you about how we barely know each other."

"Chase, we can't help who we fall in love with. Besides, who am I to tell you what you want or how you feel? Our hearts choose that for us in their own timeframe. For some people, it takes years to feel that strongly for someone. For others, it may only take weeks. Neither one is right nor wrong. Just follow your heart."

I'm speechless. *Who is this woman and what has she done with my mother?* All I can do is stand and stare, bewildered. This is not how I thought this conversation was going to go.

"I don't know what to do anymore," I say.

"Well, if you truly love her, don't give up. Give her some time to heal. The poor girl lost her mother, the only family she had left. That's a lot for anyone to handle, but it's especially hard for someone who's so young. She'll reach out when she's ready."

"At this rate, I'll be waiting for months. How am I supposed to have a relationship with someone who won't even pick up the phone?"

"You have to ask yourself if she's worth the wait. I'm not saying she's handling this the best way. After all, you're my son. But, I don't think she's doing this to hurt you on purpose. You have to be willing to put yourself in her shoes. Try to understand what she's going through. What happened to her was tragic, and now she's adjusting to a brand-new life with no more safety net to catch her when she falls."

"*I'm* her safety net, Mom," I emphasize.

"Then catch her," she says. Now I know where Meg gets that obvious tone.

My mom steps forward and places her hands on my shoulders. The gesture makes me feel like I'm a kid again. She looks like she's about to impart some more motherly wisdom on me—as if she hasn't already made her point. She looks up at me, her soft eyes conveying a deep-seated love. "I just want you to be happy with whatever choice you decide. If you love Mia, and she makes you happy, then go get her. A love like that doesn't always come around a second time."

She's right. There won't ever be another Mia. She's a one-of-a-kind woman. So what the fuck am I doing here wallowing away in self-pity? I'm a full believer that I control my own destiny. If I want something, I go after it and work my ass off to get it. Why am I telling myself that this is out of my control? It's not. If Mia doesn't want to talk to me—well, I just don't accept that.

And then it hits me like a mighty kick to the balls. I know how I'm going to get her back. I once told her not too long ago that if she didn't hear me out and give me a chance, I'd harass her until she did.

So how's this any different? I need to get her back and I'm going to do it the same way I got her in the first place—perseverance.

"Mom, you're fucking brilliant," I praise, kissing her cheek.

"I didn't tell you anything that you didn't already know," she says. "And watch your mouth."

Now *that's* my mom.

She turns and walks out of the garage. Feeling rejuvenated, I grab my phone and search through my contacts until I find Raven's number. I have an idea, and in order for it to work, I'm going to need her help.

TWENTY-TWO

a m e l i a

There's a loud knock on the door that wakes me up from the soundest sleep I've had in weeks. It's Christmas morning, and I had intended to sleep all day, until this unknown douche bag came along and threw a monkey wrench into my plans. I reach for my phone on the nightstand and check the time: it's 10:02 a.m. When the knocking doesn't cease, I let out a frustrated grunt and kick the covers off. I throw on some sweatpants and begrudgingly walk to the front door.

Strands of Christmas lights are hanging down from the ceiling. Ever seen *National Lampoon's Christmas Vacation*? Remember when Clark Griswold covers every square inch of his house in Christmas lights? That's what the inside of our living room looks like. You would think a Hallmark store got a hold of us and vomited all over our walls. To say Raven overdid it with the decorating would be a bit of an understatement. To put it in perspective, we have a Hanukkah menorah perched on our windowsill, but we're not Jewish.

Before unlocking the door, I check through the peephole to see who it is. There's a guy who looks to be around my age dressed in a black long-sleeved shirt and dark blue jeans. His hair is chestnut and he's currently looking down at his phone, presumably texting someone. I've never seen him before, and I don't know why he'd be knocking on my door on Christmas morning, or any other morning, for that matter. I unlock the door and open it just a crack.

"Can I help you?"

He immediately looks up and slides his phone into his pocket. "Hi, you must be Amelia. I'm Ethan, and I have a delivery for you," he says brightly. He isn't dressed in any uniform that would indicate he's a delivery guy, and nobody delivers on Christmas.

"It's Christmas. There aren't any deliveries on Christmas," I say, irritated. I start to close the door on him, but he sticks his foot in the wedge to stop me.

"Correction. There is one delivery, and it's for you. Mind if I come in?" he asks, presumptuous.

"No, you may not." I push the door against his shoe, but he doesn't budge. I've gone from slightly irritated, to boiling hot anger. Doesn't take much to push me over the edge these days. I'm still emotionally fragile, and it's Christmas—a day where everyone is happily celebrating with their families—everyone but me. I can't feel too sorry for myself, though. I chose that route. Raven invited me to her parents' place, but I declined. After losing my mom, the last thing I want to do is surround myself with a large family to remind me that

I have none, so I chose to stay home. Besides, with the Ebenezer Scrooge-like mood I'm in, who would want to be around me, anyway?

"Okay, I'm only going to say this once. Move your foot out of the way," I snap.

He shakes his head, giving me an apologetic look. "Sorry, no can do. I'm not leaving here until you get your gift. I've got orders from Chase. He already warned me that I might get a reaction like this, so don't bother trying to get me to leave. It won't work."

The second half of that sentence would have sealed his fate if it weren't for the name drop. *Chase sent him?* Hope blooms in my chest with the possibility that he's still thinking about me.

Truth is I can't stop thinking about him, either. I never worked up the courage to call him back because I was scared it was too late. It's like when you know you have to do well on a final exam in order to get a decent grade in the class, but you deliberately blow it off because you're so afraid to fail. Everything else you've already done up to that point all hinges on how well you perform on the final, however, by not taking the exam, you've already sabotaged yourself. That's what this feels like. I didn't want to hear Chase tell me that it was over, so I avoided him at all costs, and probably destroyed the relationship as a result. Hearing him say that it was too late for us, would've shattered whatever little jagged pieces were left of me. I've already surpassed my quota for loss and pain this month.

"What do you mean until I get my gift? What gift?" I ask, confused.

He holds up a finger as if to say "just a moment" and turns, jogging down the stairs. I leave the door cracked and walk into the kitchen to make some breakfast. I grab some vanilla yogurt, strawberries, and bananas out of the fridge, and decide to make myself a smoothie. I grab the blender from the cupboard and look around for a place to set it down, but I can't find one. Raven's homemade cookies and fudge are covering every inch of space on the counter tops. They're all still sitting out on wax paper from last night. We were watching *It's a Wonderful Life,* and out of nowhere, she got the urge to bake. Normally, my ass and thighs would hate her for that, but since I wasn't eating much there for a while, those sinfully delicious sweets have been helping me gain some much-needed weight back.

I stride into the living room and plug the blender into the wall by the TV. I sit down on the floor with the cutting board, peel the banana, and cut the stems off all the strawberries. I throw everything into the blender, stick the lid on, and start it up. The door flies open, and I turn my head to see Ethan backing in. He's carrying something heavy, so I hop to my feet and race over to help him.

"Back up," he orders. His voice is strained from the weight of whatever he's lifting. I do as he says and move out of the way so he can back further in. He makes his way through the door carrying a dark mahogany dresser. Another guy walks through the door holding the other end.

"Where's your bedroom?" Ethan asks loudly, over all the commotion. I quickly rush across the room to turn the blender off.

"It's down the hall—the last door on the right."

"Follow us in there and show us where you want this thing," he says.

"Hold on a sec," I stop him. "Let me go in there first and clear a path for you guys." He nods, and I slip into the hallway, dashing into my room. Knowing I have about ten seconds before they reach my door, I frantically pick my clothes up off the floor and fling them across the room into the closet. I kick my shoes out of the way like a soccer star going in for a goal. I widen the door so they can fit the dresser through.

"Over there." I point to the opposite side of the room. The wall is completely bare on that side, and it would be the perfect place for a dresser. I jump up onto my bed so I'm completely out of their way and follow them with my eyes as they maneuver around. They line the dresser up against the wall, and double-check to make sure it's even, then they carefully set it down. As soon as the legs hit the floor, they each release a big breath. I hop back down.

"Would you guys like something to drink? There's also a ridiculous amount of cookies and fudge on the counter if you want any," I offer. I figure it's the least I can do for them. They look back and forth between each other before politely declining.

"Naw, we really need to get going. Thank you for the offer, though." Ethan says kindly. Of course, they have to get going, they probably have families waiting for them. Feeling guilty for my initial response to Ethan knocking at my door, I think of something nice to say to make me seem like less of a bitch. I decide to stick with a good old-fashioned apology.

"Listen, Ethan, I'm really sorry for snapping at you when you got here. Not that it's any excuse, but it's been a rough few weeks," I explain, running my hand through my long tresses. He gives me a warm, empathetic smile. "It's no problem, Mia. We can start over if you'd like." He steps forward and extends his hand to me. "Hello, I'm Ethan Scott," he greets.

Feeling touched by his leniency and understanding, I reach out and take his hand in a firm grip. "Mia Foster," I reply. I look over to the other guy who I still don't know. "And you are?"

He steps forward to shake my hand, "Garrett. Garrett Henderson."

"It's nice to meet you both," I say, stepping back into a familiar stance.

"So how do you guys know Chase?"

"We both bartend at Surge. He's a good friend of ours," Garrett explains.

"Oh, well, thank you both for hauling this up and dropping it off."

"Of course. It's nice to finally put a face to the girl that Chase never stops talking about," Ethan spills. I feel a blush creeping up my face and residing in my cheeks. As much as it warms my heart to hear that Chase talks about me, I don't know these guys, and it's awkward being the topic of conversation. Especially since I have no clue what's being said between them.

"We better get going. We'll see ourselves out. Merry Christmas, Mia," Garrett says warmly.

"Merry Christmas to you both," I say, as they walk past me and out of my room.

When I hear the front door open and close, I let out a painful breath. All the times I should've called Chase, and didn't, are catching up with me. The guilt is swallowing me whole. Looking at this beautiful dresser sitting in front of me isn't helping. I take small, light steps to close the space, and simply take a moment to admire his work. It's absolutely stunning. Each drawer is embellished with an antique-looking silver knob in the design of a rose. I crouch down and open the bottom drawer. There's so much space to put all my clothes. The dresser smells like Chase after he gets off work. I close my eyes and breath it in, imagining what he would say if he were here right now.

One by one, I open the drawers in awe. Every angle is impeccable, and the knobs are dead center. The wood is smooth on the inside and stained to perfection on the outside. The amount of time he must've spent in order to make this perfect must be staggering. When I reach the top right drawer, I slide it open, and find an envelope with my name neatly inscribed across it. Curious, I pick it up and flip it over. I slide my finger under the seal and rip it open.

I peek inside. There's a folded piece of paper with a necklace attached. I set the envelope down on top of the dresser and examine the necklace carefully. In the middle, there's a silver triangle, and on each side, there are interwoven strings attached to it. On the left side, the strands are gray and white. On the right side, there's red, orange, yellow, green, blue, and violet bundles; one for each color of the rainbow. I'd recognize the design anywhere. It's supposed to match Pink Floyd's *Dark Side of The Moon* album cover. My eyes water up as I gradually unfold the letter in my hands.

Mia,

Merry Christmas, baby. I'm so sorry I couldn't be there to deliver this to you in person. I would love to have seen the look on your face when it arrived. I truly hope you like it. We worked hard on it. Yes—I said we. What? You don't recognize it? This is the same dresser that you and I were working on that day in my parents' garage. That's why I wouldn't tell you what we were making. I wanted it to be a surprise.

Have I told you how beautiful you look today? Well, you look breathtaking. If you're reading this letter, then I'm sure you've found the necklace that goes along with it. That necklace was handmade for you, too. I tried my best to replicate the prism, but let's remember, I'm a carpenter, not a jewelry designer. As I was making it, I realized something important. Before you came into my life and selfishly ruined me for other women, I was having a good time. I had complete freedom to do whatever I wanted, and I had no one to answer to. I loved it. But then you came hurling into my life, like the force of nature you are, and completely fucked up my entire system. Can I tell you a secret? I loved that even more. You are strong, beautiful, intelligent, witty, kind, loyal, funny, caring, sexy, compassionate, stubborn as can be...do you want me to keep going? Fine, I'll stop. My point is, you are everything.

The first moment I laid eyes on you, I knew I was a goner. I saw you walk into Eric's apartment with Raven, and I watched your every move. I was mesmerized, spellbound. You were this hot little badass on the outside, but I could see the storm brewing on the inside. I could see how fragile and vulnerable you really were, even though you were trying to hide it behind your sunglasses, your sexy smartass mouth, and your feigned indifference. But I could also tell you had been through something harsh, and you were durable, tough. I love both sides of you. I love every side of you. And I wouldn't dream of changing one, single hair on that gorgeous head of yours. I want you. I want your good, and I want your bad. I want it all, Mia.

The necklace I'm giving you represents many different things. One is what you have done for my life. You've taken a man whose world was colorless, and you transformed it into one of vibrant color. You are an amazing exertion of light and color, Mia. You are never dull. You are never gray. But lately, my world is dull and gray again because I don't have you. I feel like my heart is missing, and I'm running on autopilot. Please tell me you feel the same way, because I miss you like crazy, and I need my heart back in order to function.

You've challenged me and helped open my mind and world up to new possibilities. You've loved me hard, just as I have you, and I will never regret one, single, waking, breathing moment I've spent with you. You are, without a doubt, the very best thing to happen to me. Regardless of what happens, or where we go from here, never question how much I love you.

P.S. I know how much music influences your life, so I'm going to ask you to listen to a song for me. Listen to "Morning" by Beck. That song says it all.

A teardrop falls on the last line of his letter, and the dam inside me breaks. After deflecting, suppressing, and ignoring my feelings for weeks, I let it all out. It feels so good to ugly cry. I sit down on the edge of the bed, cover my face with my hands, and let the tears fall in a constant stream. Whoever said: *"One day, someone is going to come along and hug you so tight, that all of your broken pieces will fit back together again,"* hit the nail on the head. That about sums up what Chase's letter just did for my heart. I can't let the best thing to ever happen to me slip away without a fight. I need to make this right.

TWENTY-THREE

a m e l i a

"Are you sure this is going to work, Rave?" I ask.

We're in the bathroom getting ready for Eric's New Year's Eve party. Technically, it's already started, but Raven is always fashionably late. We're both dressed to kill. Raven is wearing a one-shouldered, skintight, champagne colored mini dress, with a pair of open-toed heels. Her hair is styled up in a messy knot, with a few chocolate ringlets spilling down to her shoulders. Her honey eyes shimmer with brown eyeliner and beige eye shadow.

I'm in a black halter dress that's tight from the waist up but flares out a little at the hip. My hair is down and loosely curled. I'm wearing my most expensive patent leather pumps; ones that Raven gave me last year for my birthday. Luckily, I was able to bring them back with me the second time around.

For my makeup, I've chosen to go with my usual smokey eye look, and I added some nude gloss to my lips for an extra oomph. The only colorful thing I'm wearing is the necklace Chase made me that's secured around my neck. I've already filled Raven in on my plans to get him back, and she's on board.

"Well, if it doesn't work, then he's even more stupid than I gave him credit for," she says, leaning over the counter to curl her eyelashes.

"Eric is going to fall to his knees when he sees you in that dress."

"That's exactly what I'm hoping for," she says, her gaze finding mine in the mirror. With a mischievous smile, she winks at me. I laugh and start cleaning up all of our makeup, while Miss Prim and Proper finishes getting ready.

It's 10:00 p.m. when we pull up to Eric's place. My stomach is completely tangled up in knots because I'm so anxious to see Chase. It's a good anxious, because I haven't laid eyes on him in about a month, and it's a bad anxious, because I have no idea how he's going to react when he sees me. I honestly wouldn't blame him if he didn't want to talk to me, but I'm really hoping he does.

I take a deep breath to try and calm myself. When I think about how fast my pulse is racing, it makes me anxious all over again. I reach down and unbuckle my seatbelt with trembling hands. Raven steps out of the car, closes her door, and walks around to my side as I'm stepping out.

She takes my hands in hers and reassures me. "Relax, baby girl. He'll be thrilled to see you."

"What if he doesn't want to see me? Does he even know I'm going to be here tonight? Did Eric tell him? What if he's here with someone else?" I panic. The thought of another girl grabbing Chase's attention makes me nauseous. I don't want him looking at any girl—other than me—ever again.

Raven clasps her hands around my face and forces me to meet her gaze. "Mia, *relax*. Of course he'll want to see you. And no, Eric didn't tell him you'd be here. That's part of the surprise, remember?"

What seemed like a great idea at the time quickly has me second-guessing myself. I don't want Chase to feel like I've sprung this on him, and then have it get all awkward between us because he feels trapped. Clearly, I didn't think this all the way through.

"Listen up," Raven orders. "Chase is your man. You are his woman. You are going to smoothly waltz into that apartment, find him, and remind him of that. You are a knockout, and any guy in that room would be lucky to have you. If Chase knows what's good for him, he'll sweep you up, take you home, and rock your world until the sun comes up. If he doesn't do just that, then he'll have me to answer to," she promises. "I know you're nervous, but when you walk in there you need to own it. Put up those defenses and wear a poker face that would put Phil Hellmuth to shame."

"Who's Phil Hellmuth?" I ask.

"Google him." She releases my face and adjusts her dress before leading the way into Eric's apartment. She knows how much I tend to overanalyze everything and she's not giving me a chance to do that in the parking lot.

Raven opens the door, and I hesitantly follow her inside. This feels like déjà vu all over again. The apartment is crowded, and the music is turned up real loud. There are white lights strung up everywhere. *Looks like our apartment isn't the only one Raven got ahold of.*

The first thing my eyes do is scan the room in search for Chase, but I don't see him anywhere. Maybe he decided not to show up? Or maybe he already left? The thought makes my shoulders sag with disappointment. What if Eric spilled the beans that I was coming and that's why he's not here? I cringe, trying to block out that painful thought.

Eric's voice rings loud and clear over the music. "Whoa, look at you ladies. Drop dead fucking gorgeous," he yells from the kitchen. Raven spots him and immediately grins at the sound of his approval. He eyes her up and down heatedly, and a slow, heart-stopping smile spreads across his face.

"Are you trying to give me a heart attack? You look amazing," he praises. "Come here so I can give you some love." He holds his arm as an invitation for her to curl into him. He's holding a full shot glass in his other hand. She moves forward and kisses him hard on the lips. Normally, I'd be disgusted at such blatant, in-your-face PDA, but I think the two of them are great together. I couldn't be more thrilled for two of my best friends finding happiness in each other.

Eric releases Raven and downs the shot. He sets the glass aside and leisurely strolls over to me, his face radiating endearment and pride. Before I can even say hello, he pulls me into a tight hug. He smells my hair and sighs in utter contentment. I giggle and wrap my arms around him.

"Feeling the effects of the alcohol, are we?" I tease. Eric is always flirty, but he's coming on a little stronger than normal.

"Thank you for coming," he says sincerely.

I loosen my arms and pull back to look at him. "You really thought I wasn't going to show up?" I ask, a little hurt.

He shrugs. "I don't know. I knew at the time you said you would, that you meant it. But you could've easily woken up and changed your mind. I know the last month has been hard on you."

"I'm sorry, Eric. I promise, I'll never put you guys through that again."

"Good," he says, satisfied. "Now grab yourself a drink and feel free to make bad decisions and let loose. You need it. Lose those morals and pesky inhibitions for the night," he encourages.

I laugh as he releases me from his hold. Before he can run off and continue enjoying the night, I grab the hem of his shirt and pull him back. He looks down, confused, but waits for what I have to say.

"Is Chase here?" I ask.

He nods.

"Where is he?"

He lets out an uneasy breath and motions his head in the direction of the living room. I stand on my tippy toes and look over his shoulder. I instantly spot the back of Chase's head. He's sitting down on the couch talking to a blonde woman. Not just any blonde woman—Christa. I clench my jaw at the sight and work it over back and forth. Reading my mind, Eric bends down to my ear.

"I know that doesn't look good, but I swear to you, he hasn't touched her once. They've just been talking."

I wish that piece of information made me feel better about what I'm seeing, but it doesn't. Instead, I feel a sting of jealousy and rejection at the sight of them sitting so close together. Eric's previous words come rushing back:

As far as I know, that's over between them...for now.

Christa is Chase's constant....

She has some kind of hold over him.

I let out a defeated sigh. I'm not as heartbroken as I thought I'd be, considering my greatest fear just surfaced and slapped the shit out of me. It's probably because there isn't much left of my heart to break. Maybe that's God's way of reassuring me that He knows I can't take anymore. I'm tired of always feeling like I'm fighting a losing battle. I'd like to be on the winning side for once.

"I think I'm just going to head out."

"The hell you are!" Raven interjects before Eric has a chance to respond. "Mia, I love you to death, but use your head. You're a fighter but you seem to have forgotten that. You do not just roll over and die. That's not who you are. You have every right to grieve the loss of your mom, but I'm tired of you acting like there's nothing you can do to save your relationship. For crying out loud he's sitting less than ten feet away from you, talking to some blonde bimbo, when he'd obviously rather be talking to you. Go fight for him the way he would for you if the situation were reversed." She takes in a deep breath—a good idea since she used all of her last one to get that out of her system.

I look at her, surprised. This obviously has been building up inside of her for the last month. Makes sense. She's had to live with me day in and day out while I'm going through all of this. That couldn't have been easy.

Witnessing a loved one suffer is almost worse than experiencing it yourself. At least when you experience it yourself, you have a certain amount of control over the situation. You decide what you're going to do next and how you're going to move forward. You focus all of your energy on bouncing back from whatever has you down. When a loved one is suffering, there's not much you can do to help other than just be there for support.

"You know something, you're right. Thank you, Raven. I needed that," I say, surprisingly relieved. "Pour me a shot so I can down some liquid courage and go win my man back," I say with renewed determination.

"Oh, thank God," Raven rejoices. "I've been waiting for that fire to light for weeks."

Eric smiles and pours me a shot of straight vodka. I take the glass from him and raise it up high in the air. "This one's for you, Mom," I say, downing it. I slam the glass against the table and feel the liquid burn a path down my throat.

"Do me a favor?" I ask Eric.

"What do you need?"

"I need you to turn the down the music so I can hear myself think and have a conversation with him."

"You got it," he says instantly.

"Thank you."

"How do I look?" I ask Raven. There are no mirrors close by, and I need to make sure I look top-notch before I walk over to my soon-to-be-boyfriend-again and his ex-booty call.

"Smoking hot," Raven assures me. Eric nods his head in agreement.

"Good," I say, satisfied.

I muster up every ounce of courage I can manage and make myself move toward the two of them. I'm taking a huge risk with my heart, and I'm praying to God it pays off. If this doesn't work out in my favor, at least I can say I tried. I'll be able to walk away knowing I fought for him—for us.

I'm not sure what happens next, but something clicks within me and takes over. I feel calm, collected, and utterly confident. My heart is beating so hard I'm afraid it might explode, but it's not out of nervousness—it's out of anticipation. Anticipation for the moment when I finally sit down on that couch and see his beautiful face for the first time in a month.

The closer I get, the higher my stomach climbs into my throat. It's the same feeling I get right before a major drop on a rollercoaster ride. I try to ignore the sensation. Just as I round the side of the couch, the volume on the stereo lowers. I swoop in without warning and sit down right next to Christa. Chase is on the opposite side of her, drinking a beer. I see him freeze up with the bottle near his lips. Christa abruptly stops whatever pointless conversation she was having with him and turns to look at me. A look of pure annoyance washes over her face.

As bad as this is to admit, I internally feel a great deal of satisfaction knowing I've blown her chances of keeping his attention. I'm not getting cocky; I'm just banking on him and his love for me to overrule her. I smoothly bring one leg up to cross over the other. Delicately, I adjust the hem of my skirt and casually lean back into the couch. I crane my neck to steal a glimpse of Chase.

Sound familiar? Just wait….

"So, Chase, here's what I've been thinking; I think it's imperative that we go out on a date. I'm proposing dinner and something fun afterwards. What do you say?" I know those weren't his exact words the first time he asked me out, but I know it's pretty damn close. The majority of that night will forever be ingrained in my mind. It's hard to forget when a man like Chase comes onto you. He has that certain something that makes you give him your complete and undivided attention—even if you don't want to.

His eyes widen in shock, but he doesn't respond. He's probably waiting for the catch, even though there isn't one. I wish I could tell you what Christa's reaction looks like, but all I can seem to focus on is this gorgeous man in front of me.

"You're cute when you're speechless, you know that?" I flirt.

Still nothing. I finally break our gaze and look over at Christa, heading for line number three. "Christa, could you do me a favor? Could you please tell your friend Chase that I'd like to apologize to him for my behavior these last few weeks. I believe I owe him an explanation."

She rolls her eyes. "Tell him yourself."

Gotta admire her spunk.

Chase gently sets his beer down on the coffee table and leans forward to look me in the eyes. "You know, Mia, if you wanted to talk to me, you should've called a month ago," he says coolly, detached.

Ouch.

"That's fair. I deserved that one," I say carefully. "You're right, I should've called. I should've done a lot of things that I didn't do, and I'm sorry for that."

He stares at me intently for a moment, and then his gaze slips and drops down to my necklace. I analyze every move, every feature, and every other nonverbal cue I can, in an attempt to read him. For the briefest of seconds, I see something flash through his eyes. *Hope, maybe? Or perhaps it's warmth?* Hard to tell at this point.

He swallows and lifts his gaze back up to mine. He looks so vulnerable. It completely guts me. I know Christa's still here watching us, but I can't stand the distance anymore. I rise and move to sit down on the coffee table so I can be closer to him. It's the perfect spot to give him my own rendition of what he said to me that first night.

I reach out to hold his hands, hoping that he'll let me touch him. I slide my hand over the inside of his palm and intertwine our fingers. It takes him an extra moment before he closes his down over mine. I let out the breath I'd been holding, slightly relieved.

"Do you feel this, baby? This is chemistry. You can't deny it and neither can I. I'd love to sit here and tell you that I'll never hurt you again, but I'm going to make mistakes and so are you. What I can guarantee is I'll do anything to make this relationship work. I promise to fight for you—for us—just like you have for me all along. I'm sorry I shut you out. I wanted to call you so badly. Every damn day I tried to work up the courage to text or call you but, in the end, I was so scared of losing you, that my fear won out. I essentially lost you, anyway. Believe me, I'm constantly beating myself up over that one." I scoot in closer until my knees are brushing up against his jeans.

"I need you to understand that I've lost so much." I give his hands a small squeeze, trying to undo the pain I've caused him. "I lost my parents, my home, you...hell; I even lost myself for a while. But I'd rather live an amazing, colorful life with you, than merely exist in a dull gray world with someone else."

He doesn't say anything. He just continues to stare at me, his eyes intense. I really need him to say something after I just bared my soul. A feeling of unease begins to spread through my chest. Then, I'm painfully reminded that Christa is still sitting two feet away, watching us. My unease quickly escalates to a total fear of rejection.

Say something.

Say anything!

Silence.

For the first time, I fully comprehend the depth of what he's been dealing with for the last month. All that time and effort he spent pouring his heart out, and I said nothing. He tried over and over again to profess his love for me, and I gave him sheer silence in return. Funny how these things always come full circle.

When it's obvious he's going to leave me hanging, I slowly rise and walk off without so much as another word. I force myself not to look at Christa's reaction as I walk past her. I'm sure if I see the triumphant smile she's wearing, I'll reach out strangle her with my bare hands.

I meet up with Raven and Eric in the kitchen. Judging from the sympathetic looks I'm receiving, it's evident they had been watching us like hawks the entire time. *Great, guys.*

"I need some air. I'll be back in five," I inform them.

I open the door, step outside, and close it behind me. I turn and head down the hallway to the main entrance. I push it open in a huff, and instantly feel relieved when the cool air hits my skin, giving me goose bumps. I feel like I can breathe again. It's so hot and stuffy in there, not to mention the fact that Chase and Christa are still sitting side by side. That thought alone is suffocating.

I rest my hands on my hips and look up at the stars in the night sky. Hundreds of them are twinkling brightly above my head. I'm completely heartbroken after that, but oddly enough, I actually feel whole again, too. I feel like me—sassy. There's something to be said for facing your deepest fears and surviving them. I guess that's the beauty of having nothing left to lose, it's harder to fear the unknown. *Like, what are you going to do to me, Universe? Fuck me over and take everything away?* That threat becomes obsolete after enough loss. Short of killing off my three best friends and finding out that I have stage IV terminal cancer with no hope for a morphine drip, I'd say I'm sitting pretty good. Conquering fear sets you free, and ladies and gentlemen, I'm finally free.

I'm just glad I was able to apologize and explain myself. Even if it didn't change anything, or mend my broken heart, it still needed to be said. Now, I can finally have some closure. There's plenty of time for me to go home and cry my eyes out later—which will happen.

When I hear the door swing open, I swivel around and I'm met with my favorite pair of sapphire eyes. Chase is watching me, his expression unreadable. It's painful and downright sad how much I miss looking at him, talking to him, kissing him. He looks away for a moment as if to gather his thoughts, then opens his mouth to say something before deciding against it. He runs his hands through his hair, and his gaze finds mine again. This time, he's looking at me with the same intensity he had the first time our eyes locked up on that balcony. My breath catches and my heart gradually starts to come alive and beat again.

Then, faster than I can keep up with, he breaks out of his stance and takes five long, fast strides to close the space between us. He roughly grabs my face and pulls me up to his mouth, kissing me fiercely. The kiss feels brand new. It's like we're starting all over again. Everything feels foreign, but slightly familiar, too.

I wrap my arms around his neck and reciprocate with everything I've got, pouring weeks of pain, agony, longing, and love into the kiss. I give him all of me, and I take all of him in return. Our mouths are fused together with our tongues collide in a frenzy.

God, I've missed this.

I've missed him.

He bites down seductively on my bottom lip and gradually pulls back until it releases from his hold. His eyes are blazing, serious. He gently runs his finger down the tip of my nose. My eyes close reflexively, relishing in the small but significant contact.

"Why'd you leave me, babe?"

My eyes pop open, alarmed. "I didn't," I say defensively.

"Yeah, you did."

"No," I challenge, stubborn. "I was scared. I didn't want to lose you."

"So, let me get this straight, I harass you for weeks trying to get you to talk to me, but you don't call or text me back because you are scared of losing me? Does that make any fucking sense to you, Mia?"

"Do *I* make any sense to you?" I retort.

He ponders that for a moment. "No," he says decidedly. "You make absolutely no sense. We could've avoided this whole thing if you had just communicated with me. Have I ever given you any reason to think I'd leave you behind when things get tough for us?"

"No," I sulk. "You make it sound so simple, but I was going through a lot. I couldn't think clearly after I lost my mom. You don't think logically when you're grieving because all you feel is pain."

His eyes soften. "I know, but I'm still pissed."

"At me?"

He nods, his expression grave. "Mia, you completely shut me out without any explanation. I understood why at first, but as time went on, I wasn't sure if I'd ever even hear from you again. I didn't know if you were trying to end it with me, or what. You gave me absolutely no indication that you wanted this to work."

An unwelcome thought crosses my mind when he says that. "Did you mess around with anyone else while we were...apart?" I ask. I have to know because that would change everything.

His eyes become dark and cold. "Absolutely not," he grits through his teeth. He's offended.

I nod, relieved. "Good. I didn't think so."

"You shouldn't even have to ask me that question," he says, irritated.

"It's not like I believed you did. I was just double-checking." I change the subject, hoping to lift his mood. "By the way, thank you very much for my dresser and my necklace. They are the best gifts I've ever received...besides your heart," I say, trying to be cute. If he thinks I'm cute, he's less likely to continue bitching me out for my stupidity.

He stares into my eyes, his expression unreadable. Suddenly, he grabs my hips and hoists me up. I wrap my arms and legs around him. "Don't do that to me again," he warns. "I can't do that a second time. I need you to be all in this with me, or not at all."

"I won't. I'm all in," I reassure him.

His shoulders relax. He presses his lips to mine and his hands slide down to palm my ass. He releases a groan into my mouth and my body stirs with arousal. He breaks the kiss and looks at me quizzically. I wait patiently until understanding sweeps over his features.

His eyes widen—in a good way. "You're not wearing any underwear under this dress?" he asks, stunned.

I shake my head and smile wickedly. "Nope."

Without saying another word, he strides across the parking lot with me in tow. He pulls his keys out of his pants and unlocks his car. He opens the door and slides me across the backseat, my body gliding effortlessly over the leather. When he has me all situated, he closes the door and walks around the car to the driver's seat. He gets in and puts on his seatbelt.

"What are you doing?" I ask, sitting up. He starts up the car and the engine roars to life. Hastily, he shifts the gear in reverse and backs out.

"I'm taking you back to my place."

"Why am I in the backseat then?" I ask, not understanding.

"Because you are going to lay back down and pleasure yourself while I watch you from the rearview mirror. If I'm driving, I'm going to need something spectacular to watch to make our trip less boring," he says, completely serious. He adjusts the mirror so he can see me.

"You're crazy!"

"Only for you," he promises.

And just like that, we're off for the ride.

EPILOGUE

o n e   y e a r   l a t e r

I unload the final box of Mia's stuff out of my Mustang and reach up to close the trunk. Today's the day she's moving in, and I couldn't be more excited. I've been trying to talk her into this for the last three or four months, and last week she finally gave me the green light. I wasted no time helping her pack her things up and moving her out of Raven's place and into mine. It's where she belongs. I'm her home now.

I settle the box against my hip and walk into the front door. Mia's sitting cross-legged in the middle of the living room floor, unpacking. She's wearing a simple black tank, jeans, and the necklace I made for her a little over a year ago. She looks radiant, as always. Her hair is shorter now, too. She cut it just above her shoulders and it's pulled back into a high ponytail. As I stand here and gawk at her, I'm reminded of how lucky I am.

Raven is in the kitchen helping us unpack and setting up decorations to make the place "feel more cozy." She and Mia made a trip to HomeGoods and came back with a bunch of stuff we didn't need. She offered to redecorate our apartment, and much to my dismay, Mia let her. I'm letting that one slide since I won the bigger battle by convincing her to move in. Besides, Raven needs the distraction right now. She and Eric broke up a few weeks ago. It's definitely putting some strain on the dynamic; they can't seem to tolerate being in the same room with each other anymore. Mia's worried that they won't be able to get past that, but I keep reassuring her it will happen in due time.

As for me, I recently quit my job at Surge—easily one of the best decisions I've ever made. I don't need or want the extra money anymore. The bulk of my income is still coming from carpentry. One day, I'd like to take over my dad's business or start my own.

Mia enrolled herself at the University of Texas, which is only about a ten- or fifteen-minute drive from our apartment. Because she had a year under her belt at Bethany, she only has three more to complete and then she'll have her bachelor's degree in music business. I think it's quite fitting. She's also still waitressing to help pay her way through school.

The sound of a toilet flushing and the sink turning on brings me back to the here-and-now. A moment later, a six-months-pregnant Meg comes strolling out of the bathroom and sits down on the couch. She's been helping us unpack, but I won't let her do any heavy lifting. She's extra moody lately and is constantly reminding me that she's not a porcelain doll. I know she's not fragile, but I don't want to take any chances with my baby niece in there.

"If I had a nickel for every time I had to pee, I'd be a millionaire by now," she says.

"Good to know," I say sarcastically.

Mia laughs and Meg shoots her a look of mock annoyance. Meg loves Mia and Mia loves Meg. Hell, I think Mia likes my sister more than me some days. The two have been spending a lot of time together, and Mia can't hardly wait until Meg gives birth. Our whole family was thrilled when we found out she and Luke were expecting. Those two will make exceptional parents.

I set the box down on the ground and stride over to Mia. Crouching down to her level, I rest my forearms on top on my knees and lean in to steal a quick kiss. Each one is always better than the last. She gives me a bright smile and grasps my face in her hands. She brings me in so we're forehead to forehead and looks deeply into my eyes.

"I love you, Chase," she says earnestly.

"Lay it on me, babe," I tell her.

She bites down on her bottom lip to fight back her smile and leans in for another heart-stopping, boner-inducing, kiss.

"Are you sure about me moving in? I won't drive you batshit crazy living here?" she asks, her eyes uncertain.

I reach up to cup her cheek in my hand like she's the most precious thing in the world—because she is. "Babe, I'm sure you *are* going to drive me batshit crazy, and I wouldn't have it any other way," I promise with a smirk.

"So what comes next?"

I shrug my shoulders. "I have no idea. We'll find out when we get there. All I know is I want to spend the rest of my life with you. The rest we can figure out as we go."

"I like that. We can keep it light. Nothing too heavy."

"Isn't that your life's motto?" I joke. Mia's life has been anything but easy. She fights hard, loves harder, and truly tries to make the most of everything she has. Not a day goes by where I don't know how much she loves me, and I give her the same reassurance in return. She now let's me lighten the load for her when it all becomes too heavy.

When she starts to fall, I'll always catch her. She'll never have to worry about tumbling into the abyss again because I will jump in there after her and yank her back out, kicking and screaming. I want to give her everything. I want her to experience a life beyond her wildest dreams. Each and every day, I want her smiling and laughing harder than the last.

It will happen.

I told you once before, I'm persistent.

ACKNOWLEDGMENTS

First and foremost, let me start by thanking the incredible Lisa Cerasoli. I've said it before and I'll say it again, I couldn't have asked for a better editor. Thank you so much for all of your notes, dedication, hard work, honesty, and praise. You repeatedly pushed me to do better, and the book greatly improved because of it. Also, a big thank you goes out to your fabulous assistant, too! Thanks Danielle, the book looks great.

To the various bloggers who have supported me along the way. You ladies have been a HUGE help and an invaluable asset—specifically; True Story Book Blog, Chicks Controlled by Books, Sassy Divas Book Blog, Mean Girls Luv Books, Hooked on Books, The Book Bellas, and Bare Naked Words. And thanks to all future bloggers, too!

To my closest girlfriends; Vicky Stafford, Rikki Schechinger, and Jamie Melton—for your continued support throughout the years, and for the time you've spent reading and critiquing this novel—you are the best kind of friends that anyone could ever ask for. I'm so lucky to have you in my life.

To my parents, John and Carole Lund-Smith, who taught me from a young age that I can be whatever I want to be as long as I'm willing to work hard for it. Mom—the reason I dream so big is because of you. Thank you for being my biggest fan and loudest cheerleader.

To my brother, Zach Smith, for the advice, encouragement, and critiques. Your review of my work still makes me laugh: *"Everyone in this book is crass as fuck."* From you, that's as a compliment. Thanks, bud. For real.

To Ben Pratt, who was there through all the smiles, the tears, the hard work, the venting sessions, the elation, the drunken blunders, and the dream chasing. Thank you for taking me seriously from the start, and for always sticking by my side. I love you, babe.

To all my other family members and friends—what an amazing support system—I love you all dearly.

And last, but most certainly not least, thank you to every reader who took a chance on this book. I hope you enjoyed reading this as much as I enjoyed writing it. Your support means the world to me.

ABOUT THE AUTHOR

Lauren Michelle, who also writes under the name L.M. Pratt, is an editor by day and a writer by night. She's published three other novels—*Catching Raven*, *Solstice*, and *Purgatory*. Lauren currently lives in Iowa with her husband Ben, her son Xander, and a golden retriever named Milo.

Connect with Lauren on Facebook and Instagram.

Facebook: Author Lauren Michelle

Instagram: Lauren Michelle Pratt

chasing
MIA